RISE of the JUMBIES

ALSO BY TRACEY BAPTISTE

The Jumbies

RISE of the JUMBIES

Tracey Baptiste

Algonquin Young Readers 2017

Published by
ALGONQUIN YOUNG READERS
an imprint of Algonquin Books of Chapel Hill
Post Office Box 2225
Chapel Hill, North Carolina 27515-2225

a division of
Workman Publishing
225 Varick Street
New York, New York 10014

LIBRARY OF CONGRESS CATALOGING-IN-PUBLICATION DATA
Names: Baptiste, Tracey, author.
Title: Rise of the jumbies / by Tracey Baptiste.
Description: First edition. | Chapel Hill, North Carolina :
Algonquin Young Readers, 2017. | Sequel to: The jumbies. |
Summary: Suspicion falls on half-jumbie Corinne when local children from
her Caribbean island home begin to disappear, and she is forced to go deep
into the ocean to seek the help of a dangerous jumbie who rules the waves.
Identifiers: LCCN 2017020557 | ISBN 9781616206659 (hardcover)
Subjects: | CYAC: Spirits—Fiction. | Missing children—Fiction. |
Blacks—Caribbean Area—Fiction. | Caribbean Area—Fiction. | Horror stories.
Classification: LCC PZ7.B229515 Ri 2017 | DDC [Fic]—dc23
LC record available at https://lccn.loc.gov/2017020557

10 9 8 7 6 5 4 3 2 1
First Edition

To all the ones who were taken,
to the ones who took, to those who have forgotten,
and to those who remember all too well.

1

The Game

Corinne La Mer dove through the waves. Streaks of light illuminated the golden sand beneath her and shone on a large pink shell half-buried on the seafloor, just out of reach. She kicked her feet and pushed harder toward it. Just as she was about to make a grab, a huge wave crashed down and a zillion salty bubbles and grains of sand blocked the shell from view. Corinne's lungs were bursting. She turned and swam to the surface.

As soon as she came up, she spotted Bouki and Malik, closer to the shore. The grinning brothers had seawater dripping from their tightly curled hair. They bounced up, and Corinne realized too late that they were preparing to dive beneath a wave. The water came down, rolling her onto the gritty sand. The boys had timed their dives perfectly to avoid being tumbled by the force of the crash. By the time Corinne surfaced again, they were gone. She took a deep breath and went under, fighting the urge to close her eyes against the stinging saltwater so that she wouldn't miss the prize. And there it was, the shining pink seashell.

She kicked her feet and reached toward it, but just as she got close enough, a pair of dark hands snatched the shell out of reach. Bouki—the older boy—grinned. A few bubbles escaped from between his teeth, and he pushed up toward the sun.

"Eh heh!" he said when Corinne joined him over the waves.

"Fine, Bouki. You win," Corinne said.

"Say it," he said. "Say it!"

Corinne rolled her eyes. "You're . . ."

But before she could finish, his little brother swam up behind and yanked the shell out of his hand.

". . . not king of the sea!" Corinne finished. "Looks like Malik is."

Bouki dove after his brother. Corinne swam for shore. They had been in the water for hours. Her fingers were wrinkly and her eyes burned. She dragged herself over to a coconut tree and sat against its curved trunk, sticking her legs straight out in the warm sand. Striped shadows from the coconut leaves danced on her skin and the ground in front of her. To her left, a group of little girls held hands around a lopsided sand castle, danced in a circle, and sang.

In a fine castle, do you hear my sissy-o,
In a fine castle, do you hear my sissy-o.
Ours is the prettiest, do you hear my sissy-o.
Ours is the prettiest . . .

The sand shivered. Corinne felt a tremor go straight through her body. The girls stopped dancing, and the people on the beach stopped mid-action. But her papa and the other fishermen in their boats were still far out on the water, their nets dragging in the sea. None of them seemed to notice. She looked up at the sky. It was clear and quiet. *Where are the seagulls?* she wondered. The ground shook again. This time, she got up. The group of girls ran to their parents and the adults looked around with wide eyes.

"Earthquake!" one of the women shouted.

Corinne looked into the water again. There was no sign of the boys.

"Get out of the water!" another voice yelled.

Mothers with small children gathered them up and ran from shore. Laurent, one of Corinne's friends from the fishing village, rounded up his siblings while his mother came behind with the baby. The second youngest,

Abner, stumbled. Corinne reached for him, but his mother pushed Corinne's hand away, and in one swoop, tucked Abner under her free arm.

"Mrs. Duval, I was only trying to help."

Laurent's mother cut a fearful glance at Corinne, and Corinne's face burned with embarrassment.

Maybe it's just the earthquake, Corinne thought. But it wasn't. She had been getting looks like that for months.

"It's okay," Laurent said. "We have them." He smiled at Corinne, which made her feel better, but only a little. She had barely seen Laurent in weeks. His mother always found some chore for him to do any time they were about to play.

Corinne ran toward the waves. "Bouki! Malik!" she shouted.

The boys' heads bobbed up out of the water. They were still fighting over the shell.

"Get out!" Corinne yelled. "Get out of the water!"

At the water's edge, the waves pulled back as if the ocean were being drained. She ran to the boys with wet sand sticking under her feet. The edge of the water went farther and farther out, taking Bouki and Malik with it.

"Swim!" she yelled at them, waving her arms toward herself.

Finally, Bouki and Malik seemed to understand. They beat a path toward Corinne, but the sea was still pulling them away from shore. Corinne ran forward, toeing the froth at the edge of the waves. She was much farther out than she had been when they were playing. But where there had been water deep enough to swim in, there was now only wet, sucking sand.

"Faster!"

Water splashed on Corinne's toes. The tide was turning. The boys got closer, but so did the sea. Corinne stayed where she was with the water licking at her feet, her ankles, and then surging up to her knees until the brothers were close enough to grab and pull along.

"Run!" Corinne commanded. All three of them took off toward the hill where she lived. But the waves crashed down around them, washing the sand away and pulling at their feet. One wave had barely turned back when another one overtook it and came at them again. It was the strongest tide Corinne had ever experienced.

There was another rumble. Corinne and the boys scrambled over rocky steps. Loose stones shook away beneath their feet, tripping them until they reached the dirt road. They stopped a moment with their hands on their knees to steady themselves and catch their breath. The ground stopped moving, but the waves kept coming, and they were bringing the fishing boats in fast—right to where they stood. Corinne's papa's yellow boat crashed into other vessels as it rushed toward shore. Her father's eyes found her. He pointed frantically at their house at the top of the hill.

Corinne nodded once and pulled the boys behind her. Malik stumbled and Bouki helped him to his feet.

"Come on, brother," Bouki said.

Malik patted his back pockets and looked around. His slingshot spun on the surface of the water. He reached for it, but it was drawn down a muddy whirlpool.

"I'll make you another," Bouki said as he made sure he still had his own.

They continued up the hill and paused near the house to look over the beach, which was now covered in brackish water, tree limbs, and splintered wood. A small brown object, round like a bare head, bobbed by, and for a moment, Corinne's heart stopped. But there were others, green ones, yellow ones—coconuts, Corinne realized with relief—all drifting in the water. As they floated, Corinne saw a couple of them get sucked under like Malik's slingshot and disappear.

She looked to the pileup of boats that had run aground, but her papa's was not among them.

2

An Opening in the Sea

Beneath the tangle of boats and nets, the ocean floor quivered. Sand rose up, muddying the water. Schools of fish were shaken out of the coral. Rocks covered in barnacles and layers of sediment dislodged and knocked against each other. As they tumbled, they opened hidden chasms, like a bottle finally free of its cork. In the darkness of a newly opened chamber, a gnarled, shriveled-looking creature shifted and then shifted again, as if it was testing out its new space.

Long, twig-thin fingers reached out from under the rocks and folded into the fissures of the stone above. The fingers pushed the stone, stretching the chasm wide like the jaws of a beast.

3

What the Sea Keeps

Corinne took a few steps back down the hill. Malik grabbed her hand. He looked her in the eyes and shook his head. Malik never said much, but they all understood him perfectly—most of the time.

"I know he told us to go home," Corinne said. She pleaded with her eyes. Malik pulled her to the yard.

Bouki stopped dead in his tracks before the front steps and frowned at the small wooden house. "What if there's another one," he said. "This house could come crashing down on our heads if we go inside."

"Do you think you would be better off in your cave?" Corinne asked.

"All the time we lived in caves, nothing bad ever happened to us," Bouki said.

Malik went up to the verandah and looked in through the louver-shuttered windows. He gestured for Corinne and Bouki to follow.

Broken lanterns lay on the floor, but most everything else seemed to be okay. Corinne went inside and began picking up fallen objects. She used a kitchen towel to sop up the lantern oil and pick up the shattered glass in one swoop. Then she came to a broken lump of wax. It was a figure of her mother that she had made last All Hallows' Eve. It had been broken once before. Her hand fluttered up to her necklace and wrapped around the stone her mother had given to her. She brought it to her lips to kiss, nicking herself on a crack. The stone in the necklace had broken too, but her father wrapped the remaining pieces in leather straps so that Corinne could keep it close to her heart where she liked it.

Malik picked up the other piece of Corinne's wax figure and held it against the one Corinne had.

"It's okay, Malik," she said. "I can fix it again." She ran her finger along the broken edge. It was covered in a thin layer of black soot where the pieces had been stuck together the last time.

"Hello? You in there?"

"Here, Uncle Hugo!"

The stairs creaked under the baker's weight as he

jogged up to the verandah. He looked relieved to see both boys on either side of Corinne. Flour puffed from his apron when he folded over to catch his breath. "Did you feel that?" he asked.

"We were in the water when it happened," Bouki said.

Hugo reached up, squeezed Bouki's hand, and pulled Malik into a hug. "Are you all right?" he asked. Before he gave them a chance to respond, he added, "And Pierre?"

Corinne's stomach flipped, but she said calmly, "Papa was out on the boat, but he'll be here soon."

The boys gave her a look that said they knew she wasn't quite telling the truth, but Hugo didn't notice. He walked with them to the back of the house and opened the top of the Dutch door. When he saw the beach, he squeezed the boys even more tightly.

"Everyone got away," Corinne said. "We were the last ones on shore."

Hugo touched Corinne's wet braids. "Of course you were. The four of you really know how to find danger." Then he looked at the three of them and said, "Wait."

"Dru wasn't with us," Corinne said quickly.

The door opened and Pierre walked in, soaked to the skin and breathing heavily. His dreadlocked hair hung over his shoulders, dripping a puddle of water at his feet.

"Papa!" Corinne said. She ran to Pierre and wrapped her arms around his neck. His large arms closed around her, and she felt calmer immediately. "I was so worried, Papa."

Pierre smoothed the braids on her head. "You forget that your grand-père is king of the fish-folk and I have seawater in my veins. You and I are always safe on the sea."

This was the game they played every morning before he set out to catch fish, but today Pierre didn't sound as certain as he usually did, and Corinne wasn't sure she believed it anymore. "Is the earthquake over, Papa?" she asked.

Pierre nodded. "We didn't know what was happening at first. The tide started to pull us out. Everyone dropped their nets." He took a deep breath. "There's no use pulling against the tide. It always wins."

"What about the boat?" Corinne asked.

"I can fix it this time," he said with a wink.

Corinne swallowed hard. She felt bad about what had happened to her father's last fishing boat when she had rowed it out to sea and it broke apart at the base of the cliff.

"If everyone is safe, we should go," Hugo said. He gestured for the boys to follow him, but as they reached the door, three fishermen came up the steps.

"What is it?" Pierre asked.

"A child is missing," Victor said.

Corinne and the boys shared a horrified look. "Who?" Corinne asked.

"It's Laurent," Victor said. "His mother said she saw him running toward the house, but he never made it."

A chill went through Corinne. "I saw him too," she said. "He can't be far." She hurried to the door, ready to look for her friend.

"Stay here, Corinne," Pierre said. "The beach is still dangerous. I will help them find him."

"Where did you see him last?" Victor asked.

"He was running past the pink house," Corinne said. "He was almost home."

"I will search with you," Hugo said. He gave the boys a look that was both stern and loving, and the men left, closing the door behind them.

Laurent was one of Corinne's oldest friends. Even though his mother had been trying to keep him away from her, he sometimes managed to sneak a quick swim or a race in the sand. Corinne burst out of the door and said, "He's a strong swimmer and a fast runner."

Pierre came back and put a hand on her cheek. "That will give him a very good chance, then." He pushed her gently inside and waited until she had closed the door.

"We can't just stand here," Corinne said.

"Maybe you can't," Bouki said. "But I can. You heard your father. It's dangerous down there."

Malik crouched and took a pair of binoculars from under one of the chairs. He lifted them up with a grin.

"We can help," Corinne said. "And we don't have to be on the beach to do it."

They watched the searchers walking through mucky,

ankle-deep water. One of them was Laurent's mother, Mrs. Duval. She had taken care of Corinne sometimes when Corinne was still too young to be home alone and her papa was out on the sea. But things had changed since Corinne had gone into the mahogany forest and a jumbie—the kind the grown-ups told stories about at night—had followed her out. Mrs. Duval's voice called out above the other searchers, "Laurent! Laurent!" It reminded Corinne of how long it had been since she had heard the sound of her own mother's voice. She could only remember the gentle tone of it and a few words. She tried to remember how her mother had said *Corinne*. It had come back once on a breeze, and it had filled her up and carried her like the sail on a boat, but her mama's voice dissipated just as gently and she couldn't catch it again. Corinne squeezed the stone at her neck as if her mother's voice were inside, waiting to ooze out of the crack. But only Mrs. Duval's voice came to her.

The search party had spread out. They walked the entire length of the beach in one direction, then back the other way, looking under debris as they went.

The sea slowly returned to its normal place, but the water remained a yellowish brown. Corinne, Bouki, and Malik took turns with the binoculars, searching until the sun dove beneath the waves and everything went dark. In the moonlight, the search party returned to their homes, and Hugo and Pierre climbed the hill alone. They entered quietly and shook their heads when Corinne and the boys came in from the backyard.

Corinne went to the garden and picked two large, glossy melongenes and brought them into the kitchen.

"Are we eating?" Bouki asked.

She washed the purple fruit, sliced and seasoned them, and placed them on a tray in the oven as her papa and Hugo whispered together. Soon the house was filled with the earthy aroma of the melongene. They sat around a flickering oil lamp at the kitchen table and ate their dinner quietly. Even Bouki.

That night, after Hugo and the boys had gone home, Corinne tossed in bed. She dreamt that a wave had pulled her into the sea, and as hard as she tried, she couldn't swim to the surface. Then there was a rumble beneath her. The surface of the sand scattered like spilled sugar and rocks split apart. One of them moved as if something had pushed it away.

Corinne awoke drenched in sweat, with the moonlight filtering through the window. The scar on her thigh, which looked like a crooked silver twig, hurt. Every time she rubbed its raised outline, she remembered the day she had gotten the cut, trying to hide from the white witch. The wound had reopened when she climbed the cliff to get her mama's stone necklace back. The memory of the night she had faced off against the jumbie who called herself Severine came in flashes—pieces of her father's broken yellow boat swirling in the sea beneath her, the shine of her blood against a rock, the crack of her mama's stone as she banged it open.

Months earlier, Corinne had believed that jumbies were only stories that the grown-ups told to make children afraid. Jumbies were too incredible to be real. Who would believe in a creature like the *soucouyant*, who could shed her skin and turn into a ball of fire? Or the *lagahoo*, with knife-sharp teeth and clanging chains? Or worst of all, the *douen*, with its small, strong body and backward-facing feet? And then there was Severine, who was unlike any of the jumbies Corinne had heard of in stories. At first, with her beautifully wrapped hair and long green dress, she looked exactly like the other ladies in town. Then she turned out to be the strongest and most dangerous jumbie of all. But was she strong enough to survive falling from a cliff and being crushed under the rocks that fell with her?

Corinne grasped her mama's stone. The leather-wrapped pieces felt both soft and tough, like her father's fingers twined with her own. They comforted her and she remembered that she was safe on land. She brought the stone to her lips. Severine was gone. "Gone, gone, gone," Corinne said softly until she began to fall asleep again. But a voice came to her on the wind: "The sea doesn't keep anything, Corinne."

4

Another Way

A thin body rose out of the rocks and reached for the surface of the sea. The creature's eyes shone yellow in the muddy water and caught sight of something—a shadow—far away, across the veil of water. It was shaded the same muddy green as the sea. But it had no eyes. It might have been nothing, a trick of the water or a school of fish moving slowly together. So after a few moments, the thin, twiggy creature from the rocks went carefully toward land. It stayed in the shallows extracting breath from the water, and it began to remember.

First it thought: *There was a plan.*

Then: *There was a girl who had stopped it.*

And last: *There is always another way.*

5

The Talk at the Market

Corinne pushed away the covers and squinted at the sun rising over the cliff. She went to the kitchen and looked out the back window. In the dim morning light, she could make out her papa on shore with the other fishermen. Some of them were working on the boats, others were cleaning up the beach, and a few, mostly women, walked in a line. Corinne's heart sank. They were still searching for Laurent. Wherever he was, he had spent all night alone.

She pulled her work clothes on—a pair of her papa's old pants and a shirt—and ran down to his yellow boat. He was smearing pitch from a metal pail over some cracks, filling them in with shiny black patches. The pitch smelled of sulfur. Corinne covered her nose and mouth with her hand.

"What is it?" Pierre asked.

Corinne's words stuck in her throat. "It's . . . it's Severine," she whispered.

Pierre glanced at the base of the cliff where the jumbie had fallen. "What about her?"

"I had a dream about her," she said. Suddenly, Corinne felt foolish to be worried about a nightmare. But she had already started. "It felt real, like she was nearby and I could hear her. Like she was coming up through the stones and the water." The wind picked up and Corinne shivered.

Pierre wrapped an arm around Corinne, still holding the bucket with the other. "It was only a dream, Corinne. Nothing to be afraid of." He held her until she stopped shaking, then he knelt in front of her on the sand.

"Sometimes," Corinne said, "I can hear her talking to me like she did that night on the cliff. I can hear her like she's in the same room." She took a deep breath. "You said that the ancestors are always with us. Severine is Mama's sister . . ."

"Was," Pierre said. His face became hard for a moment. "All families are connected, Corinne. It's true. We don't get to choose who we share blood with. But we do get to choose how we are with each other. It's like your plants. You prune the pieces that are withering, and you encourage the ones that will bear fruit. That's how love works. We can feel the ones we love when they enter a room even before we look up. Those are the connections we encourage. I feel the pull of the sea, not just because I love it, but because this is where your grand-père taught me everything I know. You feel rooted to the earth because that is where your mama taught you to grow things. That's love."

Pierre took one of Corinne's loosening plaits and rebraided it. "Listen quietly, Corinne. You can hear your mother in the insects buzzing through your garden, and you can hear Grand-père in the waves. These are the ancestors who love you. You are more connected to them than to Severine. She only wanted you because she was greedy."

Corinne tried to remember the dream so she could explain it better, but the images had vanished. All that was left was a feeling of dread.

"Do you feel better now?"

Corinne saw the concern behind her papa's smile. "Yes, Papa," she said. "But what about Laurent?"

"We will find him. Don't worry." He stood up and glanced toward the road. "You'd better go, or all your customers will wonder what happened to the best oranges on the island."

• • •

Corinne gathered oranges from her tree in the front yard before she went on her way. She passed the dry well on her left and the line of orange trees on her right. The trees formed a wall between the road and the mahogany forest, where the jumbies lived. People had long picked the trees bare, but the wood and leaves still smelled of sharp, sweet citrus. She brushed by a blooming hibiscus bush. A couple of hummingbirds darted between its bright pink flowers. Bees droned in the morning sun that beamed through the forest leaves. Corinne began to skip. She went past the full well and the baker's shop, until she reached the market.

The first thing she saw there was a crack in the stone wall at the south entrance. It must have broken during the earthquake. She wove her way around the vendors, past wooden crates and colorful cloths spread on the hard ground where sellers displayed their produce. At her usual spot, she opened up her own cloth and began laying her oranges out, but the ruckus of people selling their goods, buyers haggling, and animals bleating and clucking was replaced by a low hum of voices talking about the earthquake.

"It was a real strong one, eh?" one of her neighbors, with eyes like dark, dull pebbles, said to the woman next to her.

"Yes, true. Everybody was patching up this morning," the other woman said. She rubbed her dry elbows, then rearranged the eddoes on her crate.

A few vendors to the left of them, a dark woman with her head tied in a colorful cloth called out, cutting through the whispers, "Tamarind for sale! Tamarind for juice! Tamarind for sauce!" But despite her best efforts, no one seemed to be listening.

Corinne looked around for Dru and her mother. They were usually at the market early to sell the sugarcane from her father's fields and the peppers from their garden. She left their space clear and scanned the crowd, avoiding looks from both vendors and customers. Over the last few months, Corinne had learned that a slight curve in the lip might mean a cruel thought from one person, a tiny squint signaled suspicion from another, and a stiffness in the muscles meant fear from someone else. These subtle body changes meant Corinne was being judged because of who she was: half-jumbie.

As she searched the crowd, Corinne locked eyes with the oldest woman in the market—the white witch. She was the only person who had looked at her exactly the same way since the first time they saw each other. The old woman, dark skinned with sparse white braids on her head, sat in the shade of the only tree in the marketplace. A blanket spread out before her bent knees displayed bottles filled with colored liquids and seeds folded inside newsprint. Corinne nodded politely and continued searching the crowd. She waved to Mrs. Chow, who sold fruit preserved in red brine from glass jars. The plums were Corinne's favorite. When Mrs. Chow caught Corinne's eye, she dipped a wooden spoon into the plum jar and folded a few of them into a piece of torn brown paper. She sent a little girl with ribbons tied in her sleek black hair over to Corinne.

"Hi, Marlene," Corinne said when the girl got near.

Marlene sucked her thumb and held out the brown paper, which was beginning to soak through with the red brine. Corinne took the plums, and Marlene grabbed two oranges and counted them off on her fingers. Even though it was their usual exchange, Marlene always counted them off. "I like your oranges," she said.

"Thank you," said Corinne.

"You don't have any customers," Marlene added. She reached out to the pouch that was tied to Corinne's waist and tried to jingle it. The sound was dismal. "How come?"

Corinne shrugged. "No one wants to buy any," she said.

"Sometimes I eat too many plums and cherries when I'm helping Mama put them in the jars. And then my stomach hurts and I don't ever want to see any of those things. But then they smell so good I go and get some more."

"Oh," Corinne said.

"Just wait. People will want oranges again. Maybe they had too many before." Marlene took off before Corinne could respond.

"Careful, girl!" Miss Aileen called out, knocking over her eddoes in the process. "There's a child gone missing. Get back to your mother quick!"

"First the earthquake, and then that," her pebble-eyed friend said, clucking her tongue. "They were talking about it at the river this morning. The mother is going crazy."

"Maybe she just wandered off. Children do that."

Corinne looked up. "He didn't wander off."

The two women looked down at her, as though they were surprised she was still there.

"The waves were coming in hard on the beach and it was difficult to run," Corinne continued. "He probably fell somewhere and got caught in the mess the water brought in."

"But what is this child talking about, Evelyn?" Miss Aileen asked, as she scratched at her elbows. She turned back to Corinne. "A little girl went missing at the river this morning when her mother was out washing clothes."

"You mean to say another child got lost?" Miss Evelyn asked. Her pebble eyes squinted. In moments the entire market was buzzing about two missing children.

"And both of them gone missing by the water," Miss Aileen observed.

"I wonder," Miss Evelyn said, taking a sideways glance at Corinne, "if it's another jumbie."

As the word bounced from mouth to mouth, all the eyes in the market looked from Corinne to the white witch and back again.

6

The Water's Song

The conversations at the market broke against Corinne's ears like waves. The more people talked, the more certain they were that a jumbie was to blame for the children's disappearance. Corinne had already started to get used to the stares, the whispers, and the way parents pulled little ones out of her path as she walked by. But she would never get used to how it made her feel. And it wasn't something she could explain to her papa or her friends. They wouldn't understand. There was only one person who knew exactly what it felt like to be a half-jumbie. She glanced at the white witch. But they had a complicated history. Corinne tried to stay out of her way.

Corinne returned her oranges to the basket and wrapped her cloth around its handles so they wouldn't hurt her palms as she carried the heavy bundle to the bakery.

"The boys are off gallivanting somewhere," Hugo said when Corinne walked in. It smelled of flour, butter, sugar, and salt. Uncle Hugo never had to worry about customers. Even though he was the largest man Corinne had ever known, he could make tiny, delicate pastries that melted on your tongue.

"I wasn't looking for them, Uncle." She lifted the basket onto the counter.

"No customers again today?" he asked.

Corinne felt something well up in her throat, and she didn't trust herself to speak. Instead she took out her best oranges for him.

Hugo held one to his nose and inhaled. "They don't know what they're missing," he said in his booming voice. "But I can always use orange peel, and yours is perfect." He pulled out five more fruits from the basket and pressed coins into Corinne's palm. Then he lowered his voice. "Any news about Laurent?" he asked.

"Not yet," Corinne said.

Hugo made an attempt at a smile. "They'll find him."

"But there's someone else missing and everyone at the market thinks it's because of a jumbie," Corinne said.

"Are they going to blame jumbies for everything from now on?" Hugo asked. He leveled an angry look in the direction of the market. "If it wasn't for you, how many of them would still be alive to say anything at all?"

From the doorway, someone said, "If it wasn't for her, none of this would have happened in the first place."

Corinne turned to see Mrs. Ramdeen. The woman's blue cotton dress was clean everywhere but at the hem, where dirt, bits of grass, and burrs clung to it as if she had walked through the forest.

"Morning, Mrs. Ramdeen," Hugo said. "What can I get for you today?"

Mrs. Ramdeen stared at Corinne with eyes like coals. She didn't move or speak. Corinne stuck to the spot like a fly in a spider's web. "Careful who you have coming around your bakery, Hugo," Mrs. Ramdeen said finally. "You never know what anyone is planning."

"Stop, Mrs. Ramdeen," Hugo said. "Corinne hasn't caused—"

"Don't tell me!" Mrs. Ramdeen yelled, stepping farther inside and leaving just enough room for Corinne to slip past her and out the door. Mrs. Ramdeen turned and spat out, "You see how stealthy she is? Just like all the rest of them. Just like every other jumbie."

Corinne walked faster.

"It's your fault," Mrs. Ramdeen continued at a high screech. "My Allan disappeared after Severine showed up last All Hallows' Eve, and now there are more missing children. It's jumbies that did all of that. Jumbies like you!"

It wasn't Corinne's fault that Allan had been taken by the douens. It was Severine's. Corinne wasn't even near when it happened. And hadn't Corinne gotten rid of Severine by herself in the end? But all the things Corinne might say to defend herself stuck inside, burning her with hurt and shame.

Dru appeared on the road and slipped between Corinne and Mrs. Ramdeen at the baker's door. "Corinne is not like Severine," Dru said. She placed her hands on her hips, her short black hair brushing against her neck in a jagged fringe. Like Corinne, she was wearing pants, but hers were bright pink with a saffron-colored kurta hanging over them past the knees.

Mrs. Ramdeen's face turned red. "Allan was your friend, Drupatee!" she said. "And if it wasn't for Corinne—"

"If it wasn't for her the whole island would have been taken over by now," said Bouki, stepping into view from the side of the bakery and hiding something behind his back. Malik joined him. His soft, round eyes looked back and forth from Mrs. Ramdeen to Corinne.

"How can you defend her?" Mrs. Ramdeen asked, walking out.

Malik went to Mrs. Ramdeen, putting his hand into hers. She looked down, confused for a moment, then she burst into tears. "He was even smaller than you," she said.

"I'm sorry," Corinne said.

Mrs. Ramdeen looked up again with fire in her eyes.

Before she could say anything, Dru grabbed Corinne's basket and pulled her friend away. The boys followed.

"You don't care that a child was taken again?" Mrs. Ramdeen screamed at Hugo. "What if it was one of these boys? Or don't you care because you only found them in the street? It would be different if they were your blood." Corinne felt the last word go straight through her like a needle through cloth. She felt like she had been stitched to family that she didn't entirely want.

Dru kept pulling Corinne until they reached the full well. She dropped Corinne's basket in a patch of long grass and settled against the cool stone wall.

"She is only upset about Allan," Dru said. She yanked a handful of grass out of the ground.

"I know," Corinne said.

"My mother practically locked me up in the house when she heard about the girl at the river this morning." Dru looked at the boys. "They'll be locking all of us up in our houses soon."

"Maybe you. Not us," Bouki said. "One of the benefits of not having parents," he added with a smile.

"Uncle Hugo takes care of you like he's your father," Corinne said. "Dru is right. He'll do the same as everybody else."

Bouki shrugged. "He can try." He pulled the bucket out of the well and each of them took sips of water from their palms.

"Girls!" It was Mrs. Chow, running toward them. Her voice trembled and her face was pale. "Girls! Have you seen Marlene?" She brushed straight past the boys, knocking water out of the metal bucket.

Corinne shook her head.

"No," Dru said.

"I sent her for water. It's so hot today. You didn't see her?" Mrs. Chow gripped the stone lip of the well and peered in. "I can't see anything. It's so dark down there."

"Marlene wouldn't have fallen in," Corinne said. "She knows how to use the bucket."

Mrs. Chow looked about frantically. Her flowered skirt and white apron were clutched in one hand from her run. "Do you think she wandered off?" She looked toward the mahogany forest and seemed comforted by the line of orange trees that separated the ancient woods from the road.

"We'll help you look," Dru said.

Mrs. Chow nodded and continued down the road, jogging a few steps, then stopping to search behind every bush. As soon as she was out of sight, Malik pulled a shoe from inside a patch of grass near the well. It was Marlene's.

Bouki shook his head, then he looked into the well. "If someone fell in, it would be hard to tell from up here," he said.

"I can go down to check," Corinne said.

Dru shook her head. "Maybe we should wait for someone else."

Malik unknotted the bucket from the rope.

"If there's anyone who can climb on slippery rock, it's her," Bouki said.

Malik tied the rope around Corinne's waist. It was cold and wet, and its touch raised goose bumps all over her body. She tugged at it to make sure it was secure, then she kicked off her sandals and slipped her legs over the low wall. As she climbed down, her bare toes gripped the damp cracks between the stone. Above her, all three friends lowered the rope slowly. It was a long way down.

Only a little sunlight glinted on the dark water beneath her, and she felt a chill from its cool depths. The sound of lapping water usually soothed her, but this time, it quickened her pulse.

Once she reached the water, Corinne paddled to stay afloat. It was ice cold, and she could barely see. She felt her way all around the sides of the well with her heart pounding against her chest. "Marlene?" she called out. She waited as the name echoed against the stones, hoping and not hoping for an answer. The echo faded and left only the sound of water on stone in whispers that sounded like *lost, lost, lost.* Corinne dipped below. Words rushed at her like a current, so fast she couldn't make them out at first. Then she heard a soothing melody, and as her heart slowed, the words came.

Come to the water,
Come join me, my child.
We'll sing and splash
And pull in the tide.
A whole world beneath,
A world of beauty.
Sleep in the water
And dream, ma petite.

The song became louder and clearer and more beautiful the longer Corinne listened. And the water felt warmer, too, like bathwater left out in the sun. Corinne dove deeper into the darkness after the lulling song. But the rope pulled against her waist, making her movements useless. The song began to fade. She reached in front of her and felt something warm and solid between her fingers. But she was jerked away. She opened her mouth to scream, "No!" and gulped water as she was yanked back to the surface, where she coughed and sputtered, and the song disappeared.

"Corinne!" Dru called.

Corinne remembered where she was and what she had come to do. She put her hands on the rock to climb, but she was pulled up fast by the rope. As she neared the top, Hugo pulled her out and placed her on the ground. She was surrounded by people from the market, including Mrs. Chow and Mrs. Ramdeen.

"She's alive, brother," Bouki said. "What were you doing, Corinne?" He rocked back on his heels while Malik untied the rope around her waist.

"Did you see her? Did you see Marlene?" Mrs. Chow asked. She clutched Marlene's sandal to her chest.

"No," Corinne said. She saw Dru frown.

"She was here. See?" Mrs. Chow held the woven leather sandal out to Corinne.

"Another one gone near the water," Miss Evelyn said. "It's a water jumbie for sure."

"You don't know that," Hugo said.

"Better ask the witch then," said Miss Evelyn. "She would know if it's a jumbie or not." She strode off with the crowd following.

Hugo shook his head and returned to the bakery.

"Something happened to you in there," Dru said to Corinne after everyone had moved away.

"I thought I heard something. Like singing. It was . . ." But the song was like her dream, quickly fading in the light of day. "I don't know," she said.

"Maybe they're right." Dru looked at the retreating crowd. "Maybe the witch will know." She pulled Corinne to her feet. "What I don't understand is why they can go to her so easily, but no one will come to you."

"They trust her," Corinne said. "She's given them medicine and helped them with all their problems."

"Real ones and fake ones," Bouki added. "But I don't

think it's trust. They're afraid of her. If the white witch can heal you, she can make you sick. If she can give you things, she can take them away. She's running a con like every other person selling on this island."

"That's not fair," Dru said.

"All right. Take it easy. Maybe *everybody* isn't running a con," Bouki said, "but the witch is. She has everybody coming for all the things they want, and she keeps them paying for all the things they don't. It's fear that keeps her in business. That's why she is always alone." He paused and looked at each of them. "Maybe she doesn't know what happened to the missing children," Bouki said. "But maybe she will know what to look for."

7

The Other Jumbie

The four children had to push through the small crowd to get to where the witch sat against the trunk of the tree, one shriveled arm dangling at her side.

"I don't give group discounts," she said in her creaky voice. The short white braids on her brown scalp shook as she rearranged her potions on the blanket.

"We have only one question," Corinne said. She glanced behind at Mrs. Chow, who was staring hopefully at the witch.

"You can answer one question, can't you, old woman?" Miss Evelyn said.

The witch looked up. Her cloudy, reddish eyes flicked

between the four children standing in front of her. "You all again?" The witch sighed and rubbed her damaged arm as if their presence made it hurt all the more. Then she stretched the frail-looking fingers at the end of it one by one.

"You're getting better," Corinne said with both surprise and relief. But her relief faded quickly. The witch had been injured when Severine had cursed her. If the witch could heal, maybe Severine could have survived as well. The image from Corinne's dream of the rock moving under the water resurfaced, and she stopped cold.

The witch's tongue flicked out and passed over her parched lips, revealing a scant few yellow teeth. "That is not a question."

"There are more children missing," Mrs. Ramdeen said. "Three of them, all of them lost by water. The sea, the river, and now the well." Her voice carried over the sounds of the market. People dropped the produce they were buying to watch and listen. Mrs. Chow tried unsuccessfully to hold back a sob.

"Children fall into danger all the time," the witch said. "Especially by the water."

"But three in less than a day?" Mrs. Ramdeen asked.

"Coincidence," the witch said, shrugging. She looked pointedly at Corinne and pursed her lips as if she was waiting for something.

Corinne swallowed. "Could it be a jumbie?"

The witch's hand shook slightly, and a few of the seeds she was transferring from a pouch to a bottle spilled on the blanket. She paused to steady herself, then continued working.

"They have taken children before," Mrs. Chow said softly. She heaved as if she might burst into tears again. Mrs. Ramdeen stepped away as if Mrs. Chow's despair was contagious.

"Do you have proof?" the witch asked. When no one answered, she continued. "My advice is to watch the children more carefully."

"But what if it is a jumbie?" Corinne asked. "What can we do?"

"Only one jumbie will know about things happening in the water, and that is a jumbie you don't want to tangle with."

Miss Evelyn sucked her teeth, *chups*. "Just tell them what they need."

"You mean Severine?" Corinne asked. "Could she come back?"

The witch's jaw tightened, but she used her good hand to wave Corinne's words away. "No. The jumbie you would have to ask is Mama D'Leau."

"Mama juh-who?" Bouki asked.

"Haven't you grown any brains yet, boy?" the witch spat. "Mama D'Leau. She is the queen of the water." The white witch began to put her things into her basket. Her good hand trembled on the handle. "But taking children is not her way."

"What is her way?" Corinne asked.

"She likes collecting husbands," the witch said, eyeing Bouki. "You are nearly big enough for her to take interest in," she added with a smile playing at the edges of her wrinkled mouth and her nostrils flaring. "But as you have no brains at all, maybe she will spare you."

She finished placing all the bottles and pieces of paper in her basket and struggled to her feet. Corinne moved to help her. At first the witch looked like she might pull away, but she grudgingly accepted Corinne's hand. The witch hooked her basket on the arm that held her cane and tucked the blanket over the top. "I'm fine now," she snapped.

Corinne stepped away. She noticed that the witch's coin pouch wasn't as full as usual, either. Maybe Corinne wasn't the only person who had lost customers because of Severine.

"If you want to know for sure, you will have to talk to Mama D'Leau directly," the witch continued. "But finding her isn't easy. Water jumbies are slippery. Cunning. And they don't do favors unless you strike a bargain first."

"I'll do it," Mrs. Chow said. "I'll do anything."

"You may not be able to," the witch said. "Mama D'Leau is very particular about who she will talk to." She looked straight at Corinne.

Corinne felt suddenly uncomfortable in her own skin, like it was a heavy, itchy suit. Beads of sweat rolled down her back.

Mrs. Chow stepped forward. "Corinne is a child. Can't you do it?"

The witch grunted. "You want me to fix what all of you caused?"

"Us!" Mrs. Ramdeen said. "What did we do to get our children taken?"

The witch narrowed her eyes. "You can't squeeze and squeeze at a thing and not expect it to pop."

The people in the crowd whispered their disagreement, but no one was brave enough to speak up. In the midst of the grumbling, Corinne heard someone snarl, "These jumbies," and she could feel the pressure of the crowd's eyes on her back. Maybe if she did something to help. Maybe this time, if they *saw* her do it, they would believe she was one of them. Maybe they would stop hating her.

Corinne stepped forward. "I will talk to Mama D'Leau."

"You can't," Dru said immediately.

Everyone else was still. Even the breeze died. It felt as if the entire island was holding its breath. Only the witch moved. She looked at each person in the crowd before shaking her head with disgust. "Mmm hmm, I thought you might," she said to Corinne. "There are some things you will have to remember. First you will have to coax her out with gifts."

Mrs. Ramdeen sucked her teeth. "She steals our children and we have to bribe her to get them back?"

"Sometimes you have to give to get," the witch said. "But I never said she took the children. You want someone to ask, and she is the one to go to under the circumstances." The witch turned back to Corinne. "You will only get one question. And for that, you will have to do her one favor. You must be very careful how you phrase it, or she might take offense." The witch clucked her tongue. "She will probably take offense anyway. But you still have to follow her rules."

"What kind of favor will she want?" Corinne asked.

"How can I know that?" the witch snapped.

Corinne felt the witch's stale breath against her face. She tried not to make a face or move away in case the white witch thought she was being disrespectful.

"But how do we find her?" Dru asked.

"That's where the rest of you come in." The witch plucked a piece of brown paper out of her basket. It was torn at the edges and wrinkled as if it had been used many times before. With a pencil, she wrote a few things down. It took a while to finish in her shaky hand, but it was a short list. She handed it to Dru, who passed it back to the crowd. "Mind the time," the witch said. "You can only call Mama D'Leau when the sun touches the sea."

"Thank you," Corinne said.

But the witch waved Corinne off as she walked away. She took a few steps and turned back. "Good luck." Then she looked at Bouki with a half-smile. "You especially."

8

Mama D'Leau

Mama D'Leau sucked the marrow out of a long, thin bone as she lay on the seafloor. She could feel the currents of water circling the island like they were her own fingers, but now some currents were moving under a new force—that twiggy thing she had seen rising out of the rocks. It was not right. The creature knew it didn't belong. But it was one like her. An ancient. And hadn't they all agreed once? It was such a long time since then, eh? She could barely summon up the memory of it. But there were words spoken, boundaries settled. It was no small thing to violate that understanding. And here was this other jumbie, tugging at her currents, testing her patience.

Mama D'Leau tossed the bone and picked herself off the bottom of the sea and swam toward the waves. They were golden in the sunlight. Her eyes would change to match. It was a matter of camouflage, a little trick that kept her hidden in the water so she only looked like a harmless shape, like nothing at all, until it was too late.

A school of flying fish darted up and out of the water, gleaming silver and pink. They glided in the air, leaving a trail of droplets behind them before diving back into the sea. Mama D'Leau swam near the surface to meet them. She grabbed one by the tail. It was pretty. She smiled before biting down, leaving a gaping hole in its fat belly. She crunched the scales and fins and bones and slurped the guts, and thought about what she was going to do about this other jumbie. The one who was toeing the line between the water world and the land. Mama D'Leau could feel the jumbie's fear shivering through her as she moved about; there was a reason the other jumbie did not want to be on land. The people probably hated her. Mama D'Leau laughed. This was why it was better under the water. No people to disturb her. Only the ones she chose.

She drifted away from the island and beyond the coral reef. Bits of flying fish stuck to one corner of her mouth. She licked them off slowly, relishing every morsel. The seafloor dipped low, making it hard for the sunlight to reach, and she stopped at her ring of stone people, the ones who had dared to defy her, the ones who had challenged her, and ones who . . . well, hadn't done anything really, but she had been in a bad mood when they crossed her path.

Mama D'Leau swam around them, caressing their surprised stone faces and looking into their fear-filled eyes. Coral was starting to grow over them, making it look like they had extra limbs, fingers, tails, even wings. The memory of how each of them turned from warm, supple flesh to hard, cold stone sent lovely chills up her spine. She giggled. The sound of it traveled to the shores of the island, to shores farther away, all the way to the other side of the world, passing over creatures that stopped cold as the disturbing ripple of her laughter cut to their very core. Every creature in the sea darted and dove to escape her glee, but there was nowhere to go in the water, nowhere to hide from Mama D'Leau.

When her laughter came rippling back, Mama D'Leau felt it tickle against her skin, and a wonderful thought bubbled up. There was, perhaps, some advantage to letting the offensive little jumbie use her waters. It wasn't Mama D'Leau who had violated the ancient treaty. She was a victim. Innocent, even. The foolish little thing was filled with fear and desperation. So it was only a matter of time before it slipped up. Fear always led to stupid decisions. She would find some way to turn the jumbie's fear to her own advantage. It was a simple thing, really. Mama

D'Leau settled against a particularly handsome stone man with red coral growing over his nose and mouth and tried to imagine what her opportunity would look like. She wriggled with glee.

9

On Second Thought

It was a long way back to the swamp. The sun beat down on the bare patches of the witch's head as she shuffled through the damp grass and took a roundabout path that led to a sand spit. She crossed it gingerly and entered her crooked shack. As soon as the door closed behind her, she sighed.

"Yes, I know," she said to the empty shack.

She had planned to leave the child and the rest of them to whatever fate Mama D'Leau decided for them. She was so tired. It had been a long time since she wasn't needed by *someone*, for *something*. She only wanted to *be* now. But it was too late. The jumbie would know that she had told them how to call her out of the water. The witch had interfered. Again. And she wasn't supposed to, so she would have to pay. Making Mama D'Leau come to her there on the swamp would only incur the jumbie's wrath. So the white witch might as well meet her on the beach. And while she was there, she would help the child.

"In for a penny, in for a pound," she said to no one again.

The witch put her basket on the lone wood table, not even bothering to empty the contents. She walked back outside where the sun shone on her face, and hesitated.

"You must have cooked my brains," the witch told the sun. Then she began the long trek to Corinne's beach.

10

Under Water

No, Corinne," Pierre said. He shook his head so hard his locs beat against his broad shoulders. He gathered Corinne's small hands into his larger ones. "No."

"Papa, I can help Laurent and Marlene and the other girl who went missing."

"Let someone else go. You've done enough." The top of the Dutch door was open and he glanced over at the people gathering on the beach.

"She will listen to me, Papa," Corinne said. "Because she and I . . . we're the same."

That shadowy worry came over Pierre again. He kept his hands firmly over hers.

"There isn't much time," Corinne said. "Everyone is waiting." She took a deep breath. "And the witch said that it has to be done at sunset."

Pierre sighed. "All right, but I'm coming with you."

This time, Corinne squeezed her father's hand. "It's not safe," she said. "Mama D'Leau likes to collect husbands."

Pierre set his jaw.

Corinne knew it was useless to argue.

• • •

People picked their way through the debris that the tidal waves had left on shore. Black-winged *corbeau* flapped away cawing, interrupted from finishing off the dead fish lodged in the sand. Their wings cast shadows until they landed, lurking, waiting for their moment to finish their meals. Everyone looked to the huge orange sun as it sank lower in the sky. Women stepped into the water with gifts in hand, ones the white witch had told them would draw Mama D'Leau out of the sea. Mirrors reflected the glow of the sun, silver combs glinted in the light, and bright hibiscus and anthurium garlands mingled with the scent of dead fish.

Marlene's and Laurent's mothers clutched pieces of jewelry. A woman Corinne didn't know stood with them.

"Gabrielle's mother," Bouki explained when Corinne got close. "She's the one who went missing by the river."

Despite the witch's warning, several men were on the beach, too.

Corinne made her way to the shoreline. Pierre hung back when she asked him to, but he was still much closer to the water than she would have liked. Bouki, Malik, and Hugo stood to one side of Pierre, with Dru and her mother, Mrs. Rootsingh, on the other. Victor, one of the fishermen, held on to a large curved hook that gleamed in the waning light. He ground his teeth together, waiting.

Whispers came on the wind as the white witch walked through the crowd. Her wrinkled feet moved slowly over the sticky sand until the water touched her toes. She shuddered. The witch stood for a few moments with her face tilted toward the sun and her eyes closed, as if she was soaking it up. She said, "Mama D'Leau is a schemer. And she doesn't take kindly to threats or accusations, whether they are true or not."

Corinne looked at the mothers huddled together, their faces creased with worry. "They want me to tell her to bring the children back."

The witch shook her head. "That will be a disaster. You can't tell her what to do. She does what she wants."

"But what if they talk before me? I can't do anything about that."

The witch's eyes flashed open. The clouds of gray that rimmed her deep brown irises, whittling her sight down to a mere pinpoint, suddenly cleared. "You will have to make sure she only listens to you."

Corinne felt colder than she had ever felt, as if the water was washing away all the warmth and strength she had. "Why won't you do it?" she asked in a whisper.

"She won't be interested in me," said the white witch. The stormy gray clouds had returned to her eyes. "She needs somebody more able-bodied to do her a favor. Someone with the use of both arms."

The sun dipped to the water and the crowd pressed forward into the waves. They laid their gifts on wide banana leaves, pushing them out toward the horizon.

"Don't make up your face so," the witch said. "Remember: Everything on this island, everything in this world has a place. A purpose. Even the ones you might not like. Even Mama D'Leau."

"Even—" Corinne began, but a roar sounded far in the distance, growing louder and louder as a wall of water rose up and hurtled toward them on land.

Some in the crowd gasped and ran back. Even Victor dropped his hook in the nearest boat.

The white witch grabbed Corinne's hand and whispered fiercely, "Go now, before it is too late."

Somehow, Corinne made her body move through the cold fear that gripped her muscles. She ran toward the wall of water that was now high enough to blot out the sun. The wave pulsed, like a living, breathing thing. Shifting plumes of light and dark water, fringed with foam, arranged and rearranged themselves so that Corinne thought she was looking into an angry face—the face of the ocean. The wave continued rolling toward her, roaring as it came. She skidded to a stop. The sand swallowed her feet, binding her to the spot.

"Move!" the witch screamed, adding to the deafening growl of the wave.

Corinne pulled her feet out of the sand and ran toward the wall of water—her heart thumping, her chest burning—as if she could turn her shoulder and cut through it like any other wave. *Me!* she thought, and the tip of the wave began to curl down, massive and frightening.

The wave crashed down just ahead of Corinne, sending spray in all directions, over her and onto the beach. She heard gasps and then screaming, but she didn't have time to see what happened to anyone else. The water surrounded her and dragged her below. It roared in her ears and mingled with the fading sounds of shouting. Her body tossed and tumbled. It scraped along through sand and seaweed, broken shells and worn stones. Once, she felt the smack of another body against her own. She was not alone.

Corinne felt her head go fuzzy. Then the water stilled. She was floating in a clear sea. Her body moved independent of her thoughts, controlled by an unknown force. It was a dream. Wherever she was, she wasn't really there. Her body drifted to a pile of sharp rocks and shards of broken yellow wood just beginning to rot. This was the water at the cliff where she had lost her papa's first boat. In front of her the pile of barnacle-crusted rocks trembled and shook loose. Severine swam out from under them and looked back at Corinne. But as Corinne watched, Severine's face changed from the beautiful woman Corinne had first seen at the market to the miserable, twiggy creature she had later faced on the cliff.

The dream disappeared as quickly as it had appeared. Corinne was still being dragged through the water, but now she felt worse than she had before. Her fear doubled. Severine really was back. Her papa had dismissed her worry, and the white witch had avoided her question, but Corinne was sure of it now.

The water's pull weakened, and Corinne sank deeper until her feet touched the soft bottom. The sand settled slowly around her and bubbles drifted up and away. Corinne saw Dru, Bouki, and Malik nearby. She tried to move toward them, but seaweed was twisted around her legs, anchoring her to the bottom. Her friends were all trapped too, in tendrils of green weeds. No amount of struggling seemed to help.

Corinne wanted to yell at them for being there, but she couldn't speak.

We didn't come here by choice! Bouki snapped.

Corinne looked at him, and then at all the others. Bouki's lips hadn't moved. How could she have heard him?

Did you hear that? Dru asked. Her mouth hadn't moved either.

Yes, Corinne said.

We're not breathing, Dru said.

Yes, we are, said a small, squeaky voice. Malik pointed at his nose. He took a deep breath and blew bubbles out of it.

Did you say that, Malik? Dru asked, her eyes wide.

Of course he did, Bouki said.

But . . . Dru began, then tapered off.

How is this happening? Corinne asked.

Who cares? Bouki asked. *We're stuck!* He tried to use his fingers to untangle the seaweed but it only pulled tighter.

There wasn't much around them but sand, a few waving plants, and schools of fish that meandered between them as if they were curious. A gray and yellow angelfish came close to Corinne's hair, nosing through it as though it might be food. She waved it away. Other species of different sizes and shapes whizzed around them. A fierce-looking barracuda circled and darted away. Three unusually small red snappers, no larger than Malik's hands, glided by. Malik reached his hand up and tickled the white underbelly of a kingfish large enough to feed all of them. The kingfish swam off but returned a couple of times so that Malik could touch it.

It likes you, Malik, Corinne said.

Malik smiled. *It's nice.*

Corinne giggled at his sweet little voice. It wasn't too often that Malik had something to say, but here, under the water, whatever he thought came through clear as a bell.

The kingfish suddenly hurried off, and Malik pointed toward a shape in the distance. It moved toward them, as huge as a shark, and just as fast. *Look!*

The large creature circled a few times, kicking up sand and making it hard to see anything except its size.

We're bait! Bouki whimpered.

11

The Favor

When the creature finally stopped moving, its rippling wake made the children sway like reeds. As the sand resettled, Corinne made out the body of a woman with shining copper skin. Her eyes were the same bright blue as the water around them, and as the water grew darker, they did too. Her hair was long and braided in thick plaits. Some wrapped around the top of her head like a crown, but masses more fell down past her waist. Scales were scattered against her skin at her collarbone and thickened down to her hips, where her tail began. It was long and twice as thick as an anaconda's, narrowing

< 55 >

to a thin, twitching end that was coiled beneath her like a throne. Sitting high atop the coils, the jumbie towered over all of them. She reached a hand up into the waves and plucked one of the gifts the women had offered her. It was a silver comb, which she admired for a moment before pressing it into her hair.

Is you call me, yes? she asked Corinne. The jumbie also spoke without opening her mouth. She reached forward and brushed her fingers against Corinne's skin, and tugged at Corinne's plaits and her clothes. *What are you?* she asked. *Not one of them,* she added, turning toward the other children. She stopped nose to nose with Corinne, hair waving in the water around her. Seaweed, coral, tiny crabs, and even little seahorses wound through Mama D'Leau's hair, catching the light like jewels.

I'm Corinne.

Mama D'Leau shook her head. *More than that, I think. Not like them there. Not like them on land. Not like me either. So what then?*

I don't know, Corinne said. The word *jumbie* filtered up through her mind, and as it washed over their little group, a look of satisfaction settled in Mama D'Leau's face.

Yes, maybe is that, Mama D'Leau said. She narrowed her eyes. *Another one.* She pulled away from Corinne and resettled on top of her tail. *Talk quick,* she said. *I don't have whole evening.* She turned to Bouki and added, *Unless is really bait you want to be. That's fine, eh?* She chuckled to herself, revealing a slash of sharp white teeth. Then she turned a serious look on Corinne again. *Talk girl, before I eat yuh.*

I knew it! Bouki said.

The end of Mama D'Leau's tail uncoiled and reached toward him as he whimpered. *I wasn't talking to you,* the jumbie said. The ripples of Bouki's quaking body went out in every direction.

Sorry, uh, ma'am, Bouki said.

Hush! Mama D'Leau snapped. She refolded the end of her tail. The entire bulk of it moved beneath her like a slowly turning screw.

Corinne was supposed to talk about the missing children, but the image of Severine swimming up out of the rocks wouldn't leave her mind. She wondered if it was Severine who had taken them, and if Mama D'Leau would know. But she could ask only one question.

There are children missing, Corinne began. She waited, hoping that Mama D'Leau would say something back, anything that might give her a clue. But the jumbie looked at her with a half-smile playing around her lips. *Help me find them,* Corinne continued. *Please.*

Mama D'Leau's smile widened. Her teeth were as white as pearls against her deep purple lips. *Why you troubling me with that? Missing children don't bother me.*

We brought you all these gifts, Bouki said, pointing.

Malik pulled his brother's arm down. Slowly.

I already tell you hush, not so? Your mother never teach you manners? Speak when you spoken to.

I don't have a mother, Bouki began. *And Hugo is not exactly—*

Mama D'Leau's face contorted in anger. The end of her tail whipped out and around Bouki's neck. Malik tried to pry him free, but the seaweed around his legs tightened and pulled him away.

You either shut up, or I can shut you up, Mama D'Leau said.

The children, Corinne said quickly. *Only you can help find them.*

I not feeling too good about children this moment, Mama D'Leau said. *But seeing as you so generous.* She pulled down another banana leaf, which held a wooden-handled brush. Mama D'Leau frowned and let it fall to the bottom untouched. She tried another leaf—this time a gold hoop earring fell off, which Mama D'Leau attached to the middle of one of her plaits.

That's not where it— Dru began, but Corinne put a finger to her lips and Dru stopped.

Maybe you bring enough to ask two questions. Mama D'Leau tilted her head and smiled in such a way that Corinne knew she was not telling the truth.

You will hurt him, Corinne said.

Oh. Yes. Mama D'Leau unwrapped her tail from Bouki's throat. *So. What else you want?*

The question about Severine burned in Corinne's mind, but she could never ask it. She shook her head.

Mama D'Leau's smile faded. *If is only children you want, is that you get. But first, you will do me a favor.* She settled into the twisting curves of her tail. *You will get something for me. And is a good thing you bring your friends because you going to need as much help as you can get.*

I didn't bring them, Corinne protested.

Oh yes you did, Mama D'Leau said. *You asked for them to come along. You was telling me how they helped you before when you had to go up against that other jumbie. Isn't that what you was thinking when the water pulled you down?*

Corinne's body went slack. She had made only one small wish for help. She hadn't realized it would put her friends in danger.

Whatever happen next, is only you to blame, Mama D'Leau said. *All of you remember that.*

Mama D'Leau hummed deep in her throat, and four mermaids arrived, each with dark skin, a long fish tail, and beautifully braided hair. The longest one had a flashing green tail with fins that spread like delicate chiffon. She held the hand of a smaller, greenish-blue mermaid who was plainer than the first, but who had a striking line like liquid gold down her middle. A third was silvery at the tips of her fins, with blue scales that darkened toward her belly. And the last one, the smallest, who swam ahead of the others, was dark yellow, with bright red at the tip of her fins. The ends of her tail looked frayed, like cloth, and one side was longer than the other, as if a piece of it had been ripped away. The mermaids swam to a stop just in front of Corinne and her friends. Mama D'Leau loomed over them, but bowed her head to each and whispered something in a language Corinne could not make out. The mermaids looked puzzled at Mama D'Leau's words, but when she had finished, they nodded and took a position next to each of the children.

The smallest one, with her slender arms and fiery tail, went to Corinne. Her hair was cornrowed in an intricate pattern of swirls at one side that dropped and flowed past her shoulders. Like Mama D'Leau, she had adorned her hair, but her braids were twined with rocks and shells at the crown and ends instead of with small, crawling creatures. And like Mama D'Leau, her scales started to thin from her stomach to her shoulders, which were a sun-warmed brown, like Corinne's. The biggest one, who was both long and curvy, had a sneer on her face when she stopped next to Bouki. Her hair was flat-twisted against her scalp in a perfect spiral like a snail's shell. It was pinned into a bun at the back of her neck with bits of coral. She flipped her silvery tail and leaned in close to sniff him as though he was a snack. Bouki's mouth turned down and his skin paled. He looked like he might throw up. He tried to move away from the mermaid, but the seaweed kept him anchored and he swayed like an upside-down pendulum.

The mermaid next to Dru had hair that was plaited like Corinne's but in smaller sections that looked like a hundred long, thin braids hanging to her wide hips. Malik's mermaid had her hair in fat cornrows that followed the shape of her head and fell in layers against her green scales. All the mermaids looked at Corinne and her friends with something that resembled disgust and curiosity.

They babbled at each other in a language that sounded like water trickling over rocks. It was beautiful, but impossible to understand.

You know what you have to do, Mama D'Leau told them. She turned to leave.

Wait! We don't! Corinne called out.

Mama D'Leau turned back slowly. The same smile that danced at the edges of her lips was back again. *You have a question for me?*

Careful, Malik said.

Mama D'Leau snapped her eyes in his direction, and he bit his bottom lip.

Corinne understood what Malik meant. She had to figure out how to ask without asking. *You haven't told us what we will be getting for you,* she said.

Mama D'Leau's smile faded. *Of course. You will be getting an opal. It's a kind of rock.*

Corinne waited for more information, but none was coming. *There are plenty of rocks here,* she said.

Mama D'Leau took a deep breath, sucking in water

and blowing it out through gills at the side of her neck. *You are no fool,* she said. *Is not like any rock. Is a jewel that look like the bottom of the sea. Is a long way to get it. But you not going to have trouble getting there.* She gestured to the mermaids. *They can get you as far as the shore. Beyond that will call for some . . . creativity.*

Stealing, Malik said.

No, Mama D'Leau snapped. *Is my jewel. I leave it behind a long time ago.*

If I knew exactly what it looked like, it would be easier to get, Corinne said, forcing herself not to smile. She was getting the hang of asking without asking.

It's a little smaller than this, Mama D'Leau said. She made a fist and brought it to Corinne's face. *And you will know it when you see it.* She slithered closer, pressing against Corinne with her scaly tail. Corinne's skin prickled and she tensed. She got another close look at the tiny silver fish, blue crabs, orange starfish, and something that resembled an underwater caterpillar crawling in and out of Mama D'Leau's braided hair as the jumbie leaned in with her sharp, shining teeth close to Corinne's ear. *But you right that it won't be easy. Maybe you will need more help.* The jumbie peered at Corinne. *Open your mouth.*

Bouki and Dru shut their own lips tight. Only Malik nodded at Corinne. She did as she was told.

Mama D'Leau hummed deep in her throat again. She put both hands on Corinne's face and looked into her throat. She pulled off one of her scales and put it on Corinne's tongue. It dissolved like salt. Mama D'Leau took two more and put them in Corinne's ears. *That should do it,* she said. *And don't let the mermaids get out of the water. Make sure they come back. You hear? You will pay if they don't.* With that, Mama D'Leau left with her tail trailing behind.

Now what? Bouki demanded.

The mermaid nearest to Corinne smiled. *I know your grand-père,* she whispered.

I understand you! Corinne said.

Of course, the mermaid answered. *Why wouldn't you?*

I didn't understand when you were talking before, Corinne explained.

We weren't talking to you then, the silver-blue mermaid at Bouki's side said, rolling her eyes. She turned to the other three. *They think it's nice to listen in on conversations, Sisi,* she said to Corinne's mermaid. *These fish are not very smart. And look at their tails!* She poked Bouki and he went pendulum-swinging again. He squeezed his eyes shut and sucked his lips into his mouth.

Noyi, don't, Sisi said.

We weren't trying to listen in, Dru said gently. *It's just that we didn't think you spoke like us.*

Noyi rolled her eyes again.

We speak a lot of different languages, Sisi explained.

How do you know my grand-père? Corinne asked.

He saved me, she said. *Ready to go?*

Wait. How? Corinne asked.

We're going now? Dru asked. *My mother is on the beach waiting.*

Won't she wait for you to come back? her mermaid asked.

Yes, but—

Then you will see her again. Don't worry.

How do you know my grand-père? Corinne asked again.

How are we getting there? Bouki asked. *Are you going to carry us or something?*

Carry you! Noyi said. *Maybe Addie and Ellie can carry the little ones, but a big whale like you will have to swim!*

The mermaids near Malik and Dru giggled.

Mama D'Leau will bend a current for us to follow, said Sisi. *She said that we were going home. Only, I don't know what she's talking about,* she added. She picked at a shimmering gold scale on her hip.

What do you mean you don't know what she's talking about? Bouki asked.

Don't worry. We will figure it out, said Sisi.

What kind of plan is this? Bouki asked. *They don't know where they're going, and we don't know how to get this jewel when we get there. We make better plans than this, don't we, brother?*

Malik nodded.

What if this doesn't work out? Corinne asked.

Sisi swam even closer. *Then you better not come back.*

12

Light in the Dark

What little light remained in the sky filtered through layers of water and glinted off the mermaids' scales so they looked like constellations. Sisi touched Corinne's hand, and everything burst into color. She pulled away in surprise, and it all went dark again.

If I don't hold your hand, I can't take you, Sisi said. She took Corinne's hand again and the seafloor lit up. Even the dull sand looked like it was covered with tiny colored jewels.

It's beautiful, Corinne said.

What is? Dru asked. *It's too dark to see much.*

Can't they see what I can? Corinne asked Sisi. *How are you doing that?*

I'm not doing anything, Sisi said. *You are. It's not working for them.*

Dru, Bouki, and Malik were brighter than Corinne had ever seen them. The brown tones of their skin glowed orange, red, and purple in some places. Their nails were pink as seashells, and their hair drifted around them in dozens of shades of black and brown.

Amazing, Corinne whispered.

What? Dru asked again.

You're so bright, Corinne said. *It's like you light up in the dark.*

I can hardly see you, Dru said.

Must be a jumbie thing, grumbled Bouki.

Corinne's stomach flipped as if she had suddenly been turned upside down by his words. But he was right. She was different from the others. Her mermaid pulled her along. Sisi's hand was so cold it was like holding on to a block of ice. It made Corinne's fingers numb, but she hardly noticed. Corinne could now see that each mermaid had subtle patterns in her tail. The gold stripe on Ellie was made up of varying metallic shades. Noyi's tail was covered in spiral whorls in every imaginable shade of blue. Sisi's yellow tail contained intricate patterns of green, red, brown, and orange.

The mermaids took them past fields of coral, bright as

flower gardens. A leatherback turtle looked up at them as they passed. Something even larger and slower lumbered in the distance. When the mermaid got close enough, Corinne held out her hand and brushed the rough skin of a kind-looking grayish-blue creature.

What is it? Corinne asked.

Don't these fish know anything? asked Noyi.

They're not like us, said Addie, as she tugged Malik along. *They've probably never seen one before.*

One what? Bouki asked.

A manatee, Noyi said.

You mean there are things swimming right around us? he asked.

What are you called? Sisi asked Corinne.

Corinne quickly introduced herself and her friends.

Why do we need to know each other's names? Noyi said. She adjusted Bouki in the crook of her arm. *We are your transportation. That is already a very undignified thing to be. We're not going to be your friends too.*

Why not? Ellie and Dru asked together. Then they looked at each other with surprise and giggled.

If you like them so much, here, you can carry mine, Noyi said. She tossed Bouki toward Ellie and stopped swimming. Bouki began to gasp as if he suddenly needed to breathe. His eyes opened wide, and he tried to swim for the surface.

Brother! Malik called out.

Corinne pulled away from Sisi, and instantly, she also began to gasp for air.

Sisi rolled her eyes and caught Corinne again. Then she doubled back for Bouki and tossed him to Noyi, who was flipping her tail as though watching Bouki drown was no concern of hers. Bouki seemed fine once he was with Noyi again. This time, he held tight to her arm.

Noyi grinned. *Hear how quiet the sea is now?*

Ellie and Addie smiled, but didn't really seem to enjoy her joke.

How long will it take to get there? Corinne asked.

I don't know, Sisi said.

Sisi moved closer to the surface under a mass of floating plants in shades of yellow and orange. Corinne caught clumps of it between her fingers.

Sargassum, the mermaid explained. She slipped some into her mouth. *Tasty.* She held a piece toward Corinne. Corinne smiled and shook her head.

A thin curving line, a paler shade of blue than the surrounding water, appeared in front of them. *What's that?*

The current, Sisi said. *That's the path Mama D'Leau made for us to follow.*

Corinne started to ask another question, but Sisi turned to Noyi, Addie, and Ellie and said something in their watery language. Addie hummed a low, long note, then Ellie and the others joined in with harmonies that rose and crashed. Their music was soothing, and Corinne's eyes began to grow heavy. Her friends' bodies went limp, and their heads drooped as they fell asleep. The last things Corinne remembered from that night were the sargassum that thinned and gave way to the vast navy blue sea, and the shadows on the very edges of her vision that darted, dipped, turned, and twisted as if they were testing the boundaries around the mermaids.

Every moment, the shadows inched closer.

13

Shadows in the Sea

The mermaids' singing tapered off once the children were all asleep. Sisi held on to the last note as it flowed out to sea and bounced off something moving in the distance. A feeling of dread vibrated through her body, beginning at her belly and extending to the tips of her tail and the top of her head. Mama had created the current to take them all the way to whatever home it was she said they would know. They were to stick to the current. They would be safe inside it. But she never said anything about creatures that might encroach on them. She never told them what they should do if something went wrong. Sisi's heart fluttered in her chest. Mama D'Leau would not have sent them if she thought they would be harmed.

Sisi swam faster anyway.

These people-fish are twitchy, Noyi said, readjusting Bouki in her arms.

This one's making noises, Addie said, giggling.

Just hold them tight, Sisi said.

Nothing will happen, Ellie said. *Mama said—*

Mama is not here, said Sisi. *I don't even hear her song. Do you?* Sisi felt the bodies of her sister mermaids stiffen and they moved faster, too.

The low moan of a whale rang through the water. It dove into deep notes and rose again to midrange tones like a mournful song. A higher moan answered it—a baby—mimicking the undulating sounds of its mother and adding its own variation. A moment later, the mermaids came upon the graceful mammals, moving gently through the water despite their large size. Their crusty heads and dark gray bodies glided past. The mother barely noticed the mermaids, but the little whale, longer than Noyi, turned and gave them a wide-eyed glance.

Addie and Ellie hummed a harmony of mournful notes and caught the baby's attention. It came toward them.

It's only a whale family, Ellie said. *They're friendly.*

Sisi didn't feel better. She went ahead as the others swam in looping twists with the young whale until its mother let out a long resonant note that recalled the baby to her side. Sisi felt something pressing in. She looked back to hurry her sisters, but they had slipped out of the stream in their game with the whale. As the current pulled Sisi, they were being left behind. *What are you doing? Get back in the current!*

Noyi looked surprised. She grabbed her sisters one at a time and tried to swing them back into the path of the stream, but they were too far out. Sisi set her jaw and swam out of the stream toward them.

We have to get back, she said. *Your games will knock us off course.*

What are you so worried about? Noyi asked. *Nothing happened. Mama's current is right—*

Long, bright red tentacles rose up in front of the mermaids like stalks. The tentacles twisted as they rose, showing white undersides covered with hundreds of suckers that opened and closed like mouths, each one independent of its neighbors. The tentacles waved like an eyeless horde searching for food. Sisi flipped her fin in the other direction, trying to stop, but she was moving too fast. Instead, she tumbled head over tail and just missed one thick, blistering red tentacle that had popped up a few feet in front of her face. Each tentacle was at least as thick as Mama D'Leau's tail and much longer. Beneath them, the body of the squid was still hidden in the shadowy depths.

Keep back, Sisi told the others, but the tentacles had

already sensed the mermaids' movement in the water and were reaching toward them.

The mermaids angled backward to avoid the waving arms of the squid. Noyi dove, while Addie and Ellie split in opposite directions. The squid moved toward the other three, so Sisi couldn't see her sisters past the probing tentacles. She surged forward and bumped into Addie, knocking Corinne and Malik together. Sisi and Addie untangled the children's limbs and moved again as one tentacle wiggled toward them. This time Sisi twisted down and around as Addie went up.

She could see the entire bulk of the beast now. It was as long as the mama whale and thicker. Its head pointed like a spear toward Sisi as its tentacles waved above. Its large black eyes looked right through her, but its body remained still, as if waiting to pounce. Behind her, Ellie screamed. One of the tentacles had wrapped around her tail. She held Dru away from her body, looking for someone to pass her to. Addie and Noyi dodged the other suckers, pulling Malik's and Bouki's arms out of the way of danger as they tried to reach Ellie. But with the children to carry, the mermaids weren't as agile as usual. Noyi passed Bouki to Addie and managed to navigate the field of tentacles to get to Ellie. She tried to pry Ellie loose. Sisi dove and rammed herself into the squid's rubbery body. She bounced off and turned for another attack. The squid reached for her. Sisi stopped short and changed direction. Corinne's head bounced and lolled. As Sisi turned, she saw Noyi pull Ellie out of the squid's grip. But glittering scales and dark red blood trailed behind them.

What if we dropped these fish to distract it? Noyi suggested.

They will drown, Sisi said.

Not if the squid eats them first, Noyi replied.

Leave them with me, Ellie said. *I can't go fast anyway.* She pressed her hand against the bleeding gash in her tail. *I'll swim for the current. You lead it away and then come back.*

Ellie's blood was sure to attract other predators. *You have to get back to the current fast,* said Sisi. *You will never survive alone.*

Ellie scooped the children in her arms and aimed for the current. Sisi darted ahead of the other two mermaids, dodging tentacles as the squid reached up for them. When they were far enough out, Sisi doubled back with Addie. Noyi hung back and punched the squid a couple of times before she moved on. The squid released black ink and darted off. As the water cleared, Sisi, Noyi, and Addie spotted a shiver of sharks closing in on Ellie and the children.

All three moved as fast as they could, but it was too late. Corinne woke up. Her eyes widened and her mouth dropped open in a scream. The vibration distracted a couple of the smaller sharks, but the largest continued to follow Ellie.

Sisi lowered her head and moved like a dart through the water. Corinne took a slingshot from the pocket of Bouki. She used it to launch something at the shark. The beast whipped off in another direction. Sisi got close enough to pull Corinne and Dru from Ellie. The other mermaids took Bouki and Malik, leaving Ellie to swim on her own. Blood still flowed from her tail in a steady stream.

The shark came around again. This time, Corinne pulled a piece of coral from Sisi's hair and hoisted the slingshot. She waited for the shark to get closer. It closed its eyes and opened its jaws. Rows of white teeth stuck out of its pink gums. Corinne fired and hit it right at the tip of the nose. The beast thrashed and missed them completely. It turned and disappeared like the others.

Sisi carried the children to Mama D'Leau's stream, where the water pulled them along faster than they could swim. Mama had been right. In here, they were safe. The force of the faster water shook Bouki awake. He stretched and turned as much as Noyi allowed him to, then he looked at Ellie.

What happened to her? he asked.

14

The Empty Waves

When the wave rolled back into the sea, Pierre worked to catch his breath and find his footing. He looked for Corinne among those who had been knocked flat and were covered in salty mud. He raced around, picking people out of the muck and moving on with disappointment each time he didn't see his daughter's face. Panic burned his chest. He called her name. Hugo ran into the waves, grabbing at the water, so Pierre followed him. That was when he realized that the boys were missing as well. On shore, Mrs. Rootsingh dug at the wet sand. All four of them were gone.

Victor waved everyone toward the boats. "The jumbie has them in the water," he called out. "Let's go find them." Boats moved out while grim-faced men and women walked the beach for the second time in two days.

As Pierre clambered into his boat with Hugo and Mrs. Rootsingh, he felt pinpricks of loss puncturing his heart. It had been like that when he lost Corinne's mama. He said "Nicole" so softly that the wind pulled it from his lips and carried it out to the waves where no one else heard it.

Some of the other fishermen threw spears into the water or dove in with their hooks, ready to fight, but the waves were empty. Pierre, Hugo, and Mrs. Rootsingh settled into a cascading call, echoing the names of their children. They reached into the waves many times but gathered nothing but seawater that rolled off their arms like tears.

When the last brushes of light disappeared and the water had given up nothing but hopelessness, Pierre turned toward shore. But the waves became violent. They pitched and turned the boats. People were thrown into the waves. Some boats flipped. Others were torn apart at the joints. The sea seemed to be fighting them, and there was no way to win against the sea.

15

Who Dares?

Mama D'Leau watched the gifts she had been sent slip off the banana leaves and sink. Fishing spears lanced the water between them, seeking a target: her. Jumbie or not, these clumsy attacks could injure her.

Mama D'Leau turned her rage on the surface of the water. Waves cut into anything or anyone who had dared to come upon it. Roaring and spraying, they sent jets strong enough to capsize boats and dump their passengers into the moonlit sea.

You dare? You dare? Mama D'Leau screamed, and the water crashed again and again into the fishing boats, pushing through cracks, splitting them wider until the boats broke apart and there were more people in the water than vessels. The sounds of screaming and pleading and gulping for air combined with the snap of the breaking boards. Mama D'Leau laughed and the water rocked. More boats smashed and more people tumbled in the tide.

Those dumped in the water swam for shore, beating a froth, but Mama D'Leau pulled the tide to her bosom and made sure they got no closer to land, until they gave up exhausted and sank like the offerings that had slipped off the banana leaves.

Only when they had little air left did Mama D'Leau let the water spit them out on the sand, where they crawled, sputtering, feeling lucky—grateful even—to touch the gravelly earth beneath their fingers, until Mama D'Leau sent another wave to scoop them back into the water, where they struggled again.

Eventually, weary of the game, she let them scramble to higher ground, looking back at the waves with fear, the way they should have all along. She retreated to her circle of stony victims anchored to the bottom of the sea. This was how she liked people. Quiet and still. And it was why she liked living under the waves, where layers of water muffled the sounds on land, and where she could feel something sneaking up on her by the ripples against her skin.

As Mama D'Leau's laughter ebbed, the memory of the task at hand rose to the top of her mind. She reached again for the current that bridged the ocean. She twisted and turned it. Things were going well until she tasted smoke in the water.

16

Before It's Too Late

From the top of the hill, the witch watched the sea toss boats and people, then slowly settle back to its usual rhythm. It was like a great creature breathing in and out. Those on shore had long scrambled away, looking for another means to reach the jumbies that threatened their children. Those in the few boats that survived rowed slowly back to land, picking up swimmers as they came. It seemed that everyone made it, but the witch did not know for sure. She waited for Pierre, Hugo, and Mrs. Rootsingh to climb the hill. The moonlight was behind them, so she could not see their faces, but she could read the exhaustion in the bend of their backs and the hesitating steps of their feet.

"Pierre," the witch said when they reached the top of the hill. "Mama D'Leau will return them safely." She waited as Pierre's muscles began to uncoil and his fists unclenched. "But you will need to come quick."

Behind her, angry voices rose in the night air. The yellow flicker of lamplight coming through the trees danced across the faces of Mrs. Rootsingh, Hugo, and Pierre. Then came the smell of kerosene. The witch saw Pierre's nose twitch and his brow furrow.

"They are in the mahogany forest, Pierre," the witch said. "Hurry."

17

The Fire

The white witch let the parents race toward the fire. Her days of moving quickly were done. Instead of following, she leaned on her stick and hobbled down to the sea. The moon was full and bright and had pulled the tide up like someone drawing blankets close against a chill. She took off her sandals and waded into the cool waves, letting them kiss the wrinkled skin of her ankles, her shins, her knees.

"Far enough." The voice rolled toward her with the waves.

"Oh?"

"I know what you want," the water said.

"But I didn't ask a thing," the white witch replied.

"You want me to stop them. But I ent helping. Burn down the whole island. See if I care."

The witch looked back at the glow of orange coming from the top of the hill, and the sharp, acrid scent of burning orange trees made her nostrils flare. Beads of perspiration appeared on her top lip, between the white bristles of her mustache. "They will burn it all," the witch agreed. "That is nothing to us. You live in the water and I am too old. It's time for me to go anyhow."

"You have a lil' time left, old woman," the water said.

"More than some." She looked back at the fire again, then kicked up some water with her feet. "Pity, eh? The water so close. All the plants and animals will be gone. I suppose somebody will mourn them."

The water sighed.

The witch waded back to shore and took her sandals in her good hand, knocking the soles against her walking stick to get the sand out. By the time she reached the top of the hill again, she could hear the tide being sucked into a spout that shot up into the silvery sky. Her shoulders jerked with satisfaction. The water rained down on the island in a fine mist that sizzled against the charred bits of land the fire had already touched. The witch walked through the salty droplets to the line of people battling the fire. Mama D'Leau's rain was helping, but it was not enough. The fire was a creature with a thousand orange tongues roving over the forest, consuming everything.

The witch felt defeat in her bones.

18

Diving into the Wreck

Corinne knew that Sisi was nervous. Sisi's jaw was tight, and she looked straight ahead as she swam. The other mermaids followed quietly behind. Whenever they whispered to each other, Sisi picked up speed, and they had to struggle to catch up.

All at once, Sisi slowed, and Noyi came up alongside them with Bouki. *Where did it go?* Noyi asked.

Where did what go? Corinne asked.

We've lost the current, Noyi said.

The thin trail of blue that Corinne had seen at the start of their journey seemed to have petered out somewhere behind them. *What do we do now?* she asked.

Sisi swam ahead slowly, moving slightly left and right, as if she was searching for a path.

Mama has never led us the wrong way, Noyi said. *The current must be here somewhere.*

You don't have to always follow her, do you? Bouki asked.

Who follows her? She is everywhere, Sisi said. *As far as the water reaches, there she is. You can't follow something that is everywhere at once.* Sisi slowed down.

Did you find it? Dru asked.

Sisi shook her head. *No, but I've been here before.*

Of course you have, Bouki grumbled. *She said you were going home, remember? Maybe you're home already. That's why the current is gone.*

When were we here? Ellie asked.

If you don't know, I certainly don't, Noyi said.

What if you're wrong? Dru asked. *We could get lost.*

Addie shook her head. *Mama wouldn't send us unless she knew we could do it. It's important to her. There must be a way.*

Why is it important? Bouki asked.

Why would she make us drag a bunch of loud little fish across the ocean if it wasn't? Noyi asked. She gave Bouki a little slap with her tail that sent him spinning away from her for a few seconds before she scooped him back up.

I want to switch! Bouki complained.

Quit whining, Noyi said. *I wasn't going to hurt you.*

You knew my grand-père, Corinne said, trying to break up the argument.

Sisi nodded. *He told me to watch out for your father, and then you came along, so I watched out for you, too. Though your father was always easier. He doesn't put himself in danger.*

What do you mean?

Rowing a boat out to a rocky cliff in the middle of the night isn't the smartest plan, Sisi said. She sped up a little and stopped again at a dip in the sand. She picked up a few rocks and bit her lip.

Corinne thought about the night she had taken her papa's yellow boat to rescue her mama's necklace from Severine. The rocks were huge and sharp and the current was strong. She had been sure she would crash. But then something had pushed her boat out of danger. *It was you who helped me that night?*

Sisi nodded. *I should not have. We are not supposed to interfere. But I promised your grand-père, and I keep my promises.*

How did he save you?

Sisi darted ahead again. *I was caught in his nets. He could have kept me, but he cut me out. He didn't even ask for a favor. Not then, anyway. Years later his boat overturned in a storm and broke apart far from land. He tried to swim against the wind and waves but they were too strong. When he went down, I swam to him and touched his hand. He asked me to protect his family always, but he said to let him go. He said it was his time. I didn't know what that meant until after I did what he asked.*

My papa always said that I would be safe on the water, that Grand-père was—

King of the fish-folk? Sisi laughed bubbles. *He isn't, you know. There is no such thing. Mama D'Leau rules the water. You land fish have such silly ideas.*

Corinne looked at her friends, surrounded by water, able to breathe, to talk, and being ferried by a bunch of mermaids across the entire ocean. She laughed too. *No such thing.*

As she said it, the water warmed, and Sisi's mood brightened. She and the other mermaids darted around quietly. A soft morning light broke through the water and filtered down to them. The rays reflected off specks of sand and debris that floated in the water around them.

I remember a ship, Sisi said.

Ellie moved closer, leaving scales in her wake. *Yes,* she said. *We were all on it.*

How? Bouki asked. *Don't you mean swimming around it?* The mermaids didn't respond.

Here, Addie said, pulling Malik down with her. She used her tail to dust off rows of wood covered in sand.

Sisi let go of Corinne's and Dru's hands and swam off. The girls tried to follow her, but Sisi was too fast and Corinne felt her lungs begin to burn. She pushed through the water after the mermaid as darkness began to close in around the edges of her vision until she could barely see. But Sisi stopped suddenly, and Corinne and Dru grabbed her tail. Corinne dug her fingers into the mermaid as Dru wrapped her arms around Sisi's waist. A rush of air filled Corinne's lungs and her vision cleared.

The mermaid dipped down to the sand, stirring it up with her tail. The pressure of so much water pushing down on Corinne made her ears hurt.

It was darker down here, but Corinne still saw in bold color. The mermaids swam slowly toward a large, broken ship partially buried under the sand. It was studded with barnacles, and waving seaweed grew between the boards. They swam over the ship and through the open hull as frightened fish spilled out. There were ancient crates and casks, some open and some sealed shut. Bottles filled with dark liquid were strewn on the seafloor, and broken ones jutted out of the sand. Sisi stopped to touch a few of them. The mermaids continued to dive through the wreck, exploring. Bouki showed a slip of paper to Noyi, who squinted at it. Malik tugged Addie toward a rotting trunk with a lid they could pry open. Ellie moved more slowly. A trail of her scales followed her looping arcs as she found a small silver box and what looked like a gold button and tried to rub them clean with her fingers.

Sisi, Corinne, and Dru found lanterns, plates, spoons and forks, and barrels for food that had long since rotted or been carried away by the waves or grateful fish. In one small cabin, there was a table and books filled with words none of them understood. Most of the books' pages had fused together, but one volume had opened to a page of long lists containing words and numbers, though the ink was faded and blurred. Inside the table's drawer was a black pouch that Corinne dropped into Sisi's outstretched palm.

Inside were coins blackened with age. They were mostly lopsided, as if someone had hammered each one out by hand, trying to make them as round as they could but never quite getting it right. On two of the coins a pair of doves faced each other with wavy lines between them. The other side was a hammered, uneven finish. Corinne and Dru each put one in their pockets.

The mermaids began to laugh and chatter as they pulled Corinne and her friends through the broken ship, discovering more of the buried treasure. They found delicate cups that they tossed at each other and plates to fling back. Malik and Addie took a couple of the utensils and beat a hasty rhythm on the hull. The muted thunk of the spoons changed to a light clang as they moved to another part of the ship. Sisi and the girls swam toward the sound.

A square opening led even deeper into the ship, below the surface of the sand. Sisi clasped the sides of the small portal as if she needed a moment to think. Addie bumped into her and landed on a piece of rusted chain. It must have been what she and Malik had hit a moment before.

It's heavy, Malik said, trying to pull the chain up.

Addie hit it again with her spoon, but when the sound rang out, the spoon broke apart in her hand and her smile disappeared. Sisi dove into the dark belly of the ship. There, crushed boards pushed up at odd angles through the soft ocean floor, but the sides remained nearly intact. Beams curved over their heads like the arches of a church. Evenly spaced along the beams were large, round circles of iron from which more chains hung. They were so heavy and stiff with rust, they didn't move when Corinne touched them. Sisi pulled one of the chains. It was huge in her hands, and it groaned and screeched as the rough, rusted links rubbed against each other. Sisi kept pulling until the links stuck on something beneath the sand.

By then the other mermaids had joined them, and they huddled in a circle, waiting to see what would come up. Corinne unclasped one of her hands and helped Sisi pull, but the chain wouldn't budge. All of them lined up and pulled until the chain snapped, sending up a cloud of sand and red flecks of rust. When the sand settled, they saw the end of the chain: a round iron clasp with a hinge. The clasp was large enough to close around a wrist.

Below it, a white rock protruded from the sand. Corinne reached for it, fitting her finger into a groove at the top that reminded her of the curve in her mother's stone. Only it wasn't as hard, and something about it sent a chill through her body. She dug around and uncovered more of the rock. It was long and white and still entangled in another part of the chain. When she pulled, it came free. Startled, Corinne let go, and it hovered in the water in front of them before slowly settling back to the sand.

Not a rock. A bone.

Corinne lurched back and away from the bone, landing against Sisi, who gripped her arm.

They took us, Sisi said. She squinted as if she was trying to squeeze the memory out.

They captured us from our homes, said Noyi. *They chained us.* She dropped the chain in her hand, recoiling as if it had stung her. *I was called Ozigbodi,* she said. *That was my name then.*

Addie ran her hand along one of the curved arches of the ship. Malik scrambled after her and got ahold of her fin. *I touched here, and someone called out Gzifa! That was me. I turned around and saw them crumple on land, watching me be taken away.*

How could you walk? Bouki asked, holding on to Noyi's shoulders as she moved slowly through the cavernous hold.

Sisi took Ellie's hand in her own and looked at the markings on their wrists, which Corinne had not noticed before. Sisi traced the lines gently, then touched the shackles on the iron chains—just the right thickness and curve to have made the scar. *My name was Boahinmaa,* Sisi said to Corinne. A little smile played at the edges of her lips, but it did not reach her eyes. *They took us away.*

But we are back now, Noyi said.

The mermaids made a circle around the silent bone, their eyes closed, holding hands with each other and each of the children. Sisi's nails dug into Corinne's flesh.

Corinne heard the roar of wind. She looked around to see if anyone else had heard it too, but the other mermaids were still. Her friends looked worried.

What's happening? Dru asked.

I think they are remembering something, Corinne said. *And I think I can see it. Can you?*

Corinne closed her eyes.

A steel-gray sky loomed above her from a small square opening and rain whipped her face. The growl of wind grew louder, and then came the rumble of thunder. There was a crack of timber as the ship began to break apart. People were all around her, lying like she was, packed close, skin to skin. Water came through the opening and sloshed over her. It covered her face and made it almost impossible to breathe, but she could not get up. Her hands and feet were bound in iron. The water rolled away and the sounds of screaming voices and screeching chains filled her ears. The ship cracked and ripped at the joints, then sank. Water closed over them. It sealed them in like an iron box. There was a low moan and a loud pop and the beam she was attached to broke away and pitched in the current. Corinne could see the wide, frightened eyes of others below her who were still chained to the ship.

Their mouths opened, sucking for air that would never come.

Corinne opened her eyes. Her friends and the mermaids surrounded her. Their faces were soft and peaceful. It took a few moments for her heartbeat to slow and for her muscles to relax. What she had seen had not happened to her. But it had happened to someone. The mermaids had shown her the last moments of this ship.

Corinne tried to shake the images she'd just seen out of her mind: the cracking boards, the chains, and most of all, the people who had drowned in the wreck. She felt a hand squeezing her own: Malik. Even before he asked, *What did you see?* she knew his question. She had grown accustomed to reading his expressions.

They drowned, she said. *Right here in this ship.*

Then how did they get like this? Bouki asked.

Maybe Mama D'Leau saved them, said Corinne.

That doesn't sound like Mama D'Leau, Bouki said. *She's not the saving kind.*

Dru chewed on her bottom lip, silent.

What is it? Corinne asked.

Dru shook her head.

Just say it, Corinne said.

We can never see the things you see, Dru said.

Corinne felt anger prickle on her skin. *You wouldn't have wanted to see this,* she said.

Dru lowered her head and said nothing else.

< 95 >

Corinne wanted to get out of the ship and away from the memory the mermaids had shared with her, and the confused, angry feeling that Dru had stirred up in her stomach like a sour dish. But Sisi and Addie gripped her hands and as much as she struggled, she could not pull them away. Eventually, the mermaids opened their eyes and looked around as if they had just woken from a nightmare.

We were here, Noyi said. *You were right next to me, Ababuo!* she said to Ellie.

I remember, Ellie said, shuddering.

Sisi continued around the cargo hold, dragging Corinne with her and shuddering each time she touched another surface, as though every brush of her fingers awakened another terrible memory. *There were so many others,* she said. She pulled Corinne closer and left the ship through the small square door, cringing away from the edges.

The others followed. This time, they didn't look for the current. They seemed to know exactly where they needed to go. The seafloor rose. When the surface was close enough that they could all see the rays of sunlight piercing through the tops of the waves, the mermaids' faces became joyful and they darted off so quickly that they dropped Corinne and her friends, leaving them to struggle to the surface on their own.

Bouki and Malik swam up, leaving masses of bubbles in their wake. Corinne was close behind, but Dru began to fall back. When Corinne turned to look at her, Dru's face looked like those of the people in the mermaids' memory, the ones who never made it to the surface. Corinne stopped kicking long enough for Dru to float up to her, then she put an arm around her friend's waist and tried to tow her. The effort slowed her down. Corinne's lungs felt like they would burst open.

They were almost there. Corinne felt sunlight on her skin. But pain stabbed at her chest and echoed throughout her body. Hoping she was close enough, she stopped kicking and let her body float upward. Her vision dimmed at the edges, going black. Was this what happened to Laurent and Marlene and Gabrielle?

19

Home

With her eyesight dimming, Corinne was barely able to make out the pair of shadows that charged at her and Dru from above. She felt sure she would soon be in the belly of some fish. But the shadows swam under them and pushed Corinne and Dru to the surface. They gulped air. Bouki and Malik broke the water after them, panting.

"They are heavier than they look, right, brother?" Bouki said.

Malik nodded.

"We thought you were done for," Bouki added.

"I thought you were a shark," Corinne said once she caught her breath.

"Where are we?" Dru asked.

Corinne looked toward the unfamiliar shore, still a long swim away. She had never seen land stretch out so far. Malik started swimming for the beach. The others followed. It seemed like an hour before they arrived on the golden sand dotted with coconut trees, scrub, and grass. To their left stood a building like a huge sand castle. It was thick, and solid, and loomed over the sea like a sentinel.

"It's a fort," Bouki said. "I've seen one of those before."

"Where?" Corinne asked.

"On the other side of the island."

"Is that where we are?" Dru asked hopefully.

Malik shook his head.

"This is different. And bigger. Much bigger."

"It's morning," Corinne said. "It wouldn't have taken all night to get to the other side of the island."

"And that's not where the sun would come up," Bouki added.

"We have to find the mermaids," Corinne said.

Malik pointed at a thin rivulet that emptied into the sea, shallow enough to show the trail of mermaid tails going up and over the sandbar. On the other side, the bottom dropped again into a calm, clear pool. Past an outgrowth of bushes that grew out of the water, they heard voices tinkling like rain on a tin roof. The mermaids were on the other side.

Corinne thrashed through the bushes and grabbed Sisi by the arm. "You left us to drown."

"You don't look drowned," Noyi said.

"Please don't talk about drowning," Ellie said. She looked as if she might cry. Addie put her arms around Ellie's shoulders and patted her head.

Sisi looked confused for a moment. "You are still here?" she asked. "But this is not your home."

"No, Sisi, it isn't," Corinne said. "You were supposed to bring us here safely."

"Where are we?" Dru asked.

"Ghana," Sisi said. "And my name is Boahinmaa."

"I don't care where we are or what you're called," Bouki said. "We are only here to get Mama D'Leau's jewel. Then you have to take us back."

"Back where?" Sisi asked.

Malik pointed across the waves.

"Back home," Corinne said.

"But this is our home and our people are here," Ellie said.

"Don't bother, Ababuo," said Noyi. "They don't care about our families."

Corinne moved into the circle of mermaids, who had turned back to their chatter. "Mama D'Leau sent us here," she said. "And since this is your home, you should be able to tell us how to get the jewel, right?"

"Jewel?" Sisi said.

"Yes. A big stone like this." Bouki held up a fist.

"There are plenty of stones around here," Noyi said impatiently. "Take any one of them and go." Her lips curled and her eyes narrowed. "Who thinks about stones when we just got back home? Selfish."

"It's not just any stone," Dru said. "Why don't you remember what Mama D'Leau said?"

"Who?" Sisi asked.

Bouki sucked his teeth long and hard, *chuuuppps.*

Malik walked onto shore and climbed a sharp embankment. Corinne and Dru followed. They were near a dirt road very much like the one that led from the fishing village to the market on their island. Only this road was reddish, not the deep brown they were used to. Vendors were set up along the sides, selling things from stalls. There was jewelry made with beads and hammered metal, carvings of masks and animals with long horns that Corinne had never seen before. A silver radio blasted out music with a quick, catchy rhythm. Corinne recognized only some of the words.

The collection of sellers reminded her of the market at home, with more men and the people in different clothing. Women on their island wore bright colored skirts that gathered at the waist. Here the skirts were covered in colorful tessellating patterns that made Corinne feel dizzy. Some wore white blouses like the women on the island, but others had blouses in the same patterns as their skirts. And still others wore great breezy dresses that hung straight from their shoulders to their ankles with large sleeves that caught the wind. Most of the women wore head ties, like the women at home, only these were elaborately folded into large bows and accordion-shaped fans, like fabric crowns. The women without head ties had beautifully braided hair, just like the mermaids. The braids spiraled out, or were ruler-straight, or defied gravity, moving from the nape of their necks to the top of their heads where they spilled down again like fountains. The men wore clothes just as bright. Their short tunics—some in patterned cloth, others in solid colors with embroidery stitched at the hem and sleeves—hung over dark pants.

Behind the people stood painted buildings that were probably once as vibrant as their clothing but were now weather-beaten from the seawater and sand, showing bare wood in places. On one plastered wall a sun-bleached image of a woman with loose, thick hair that fell past her shoulders smiled out at passersby despite the two large snakes wound around her neck. Beneath the painting was written *Mami Wata*.

Noise rumbled underneath the vendors' music, the sounds of people talking, buying, selling, and greeting each other in a language Corinne didn't understand. One lady walked close to their hiding spot, a woven basket on her head and a baby sucking its fist wrapped in bright cloth against her hip. They ducked so the woman wouldn't see them and peeked over the top again after she passed. Spotting them, the baby waved its soggy fist and smiled a toothless greeting.

A mouthwatering medley of the scents of fried food filled the morning air. Women sat behind huge silver pots atop shiny metal stands filled with burning coal. One of them was rolling dough between her palms and dropping it into hot oil. Corinne recognized the salty, inviting scent of one of her favorite foods, accra, saltfish rolled in dough and fried in oil.

"I'm starving," Bouki said.

Corinne's stomach growled, but she waved him away.

"If I—we—don't eat something soon, we won't survive long enough to find this jewel," he complained.

"I'm sure they don't deal with people who have no money," Corinne said.

Bouki snorted. "When has that ever been a problem?" He looked at Malik and they stretched their fingers and smiled as if they could already taste the food.

"Don't," Dru said. "You can't steal. It's not right."

"It's not right to starve," Bouki said. "They will be happy to know they are helping hungry children."

"So we should ask them," Dru said.

"Ask?" Bouki looked shocked. "It's so much easier when they give without knowing. It has one hundred percent success and zero waiting and hoping." The boys looked through the reeds at the top of the bank.

"Dru is right. We should ask," Corinne said.

"It will limit your success and likely your portion," Bouki said glumly. "And who knows how long we will be here."

In the water beneath them, the mermaids huddled together talking in a combination of tongues. It sounded like the language of people on the other side of the mound mixed with English and the watery language the mermaids had used in the ocean.

"What do we do now?" Dru asked them.

Noyi rolled her eyes. "You could ask for help. What a bunch of lazy fish! We brought them here and they can't walk a few steps to find what they are looking for!"

Ellie put her hands to her face. "I remember walking when we lived here. I remember the mud through my toes and rough bark against my skin when I climbed trees," she said. "I didn't live in the water."

"How did we come to be like this?" Addie asked. "We were just like them with their two tails." It was Ellie's turn to wipe her friend's tears and pat her on the back.

"Whatever happened to you, it's not our fault," Bouki said.

"Whose then?" Dru whispered.

Something prickled in Corinne's mind. Mama D'Leau had warned her to bring the mermaids back, as if she knew that they might not want to return. And Mama D'Leau knew that they were going home. She had told them so.

How had she known? Bouki was right. This jumbie didn't seem like the kind to have saved the girls, but how else could they be in her care if she had not helped them? So many others had been left behind.

Corinne's mind was a tangled mess, each new thought a knot that she couldn't pick loose. How to find the jewel, how to get back home, who the mermaids really were. Most troubling of all was the mystery of where Laurent, Marlene, and Gabrielle had disappeared to, and what Mama D'Leau had to do with it all.

20

Girl and Goddess

They needed to eat. That was something Corinne could take care of. She squeezed the water from her hair and tried to get it out of her face so she could see better. Most of her plaits had come undone, and her thick hair hung around her shoulders. How the mermaids maintained their perfect coils and cornrows living under the sea, she did not know.

Malik pointed out a small boy who was sitting with the woman making accra. Corinne stared at him until he looked around nervously and spotted Corinne's face peeking through the grass. She waved him over, and he skipped with a wide smile across his face and dark, curious eyes.

"Unh?"

"Hello? What's your name?" Corinne asked.

"You speak English," the boy said. "No Twi?"

Corinne shook her head.

"You must be from far," the boy said. "I heard some schools only let the students speak English, English, English until they forget their own language. Don't feel bad. I learn English in school, too."

Corinne stuck her hand out. "I'm Corinne."

"My name is Kahiri." The boy shook her hand. A slim beaded bracelet spun on his wrist.

"Kahiri, I would like to buy some accra from you."

The boy frowned. "You can't buy Accra, but you can go there," he said. His voice was melodious and sweet.

"I mean those," Corinne said, pointing to the woman's large pot.

"Why would you call them Accra?" Kahiri looked at Corinne sideways. "They make those saltfish cakes in Accra, too, but they are not as good as my ma's."

"Whatever they call them, can we have some?" Bouki said.

The boy strained his neck to see beyond Corinne. "How many do you want?" he asked.

"Twelve," Corinne said.

"You will have to pay me first." Kahiri put out his hand.

"I don't have any money," Corinne said. "But I can

show you something that you have never seen before. Only, you have to keep it a secret."

"And what will my ma do if I give away her food? How will we live? Nothing you can show me is worth money in my pocket."

Corinne stepped aside so the boy could see the mermaids swimming below them. His mouth went slack and his eyes gleamed. "You can take a closer look when you bring the accra," Corinne said.

"They're called saltfish cakes," Kahiri whispered. "But I still can't get food from my ma without money."

"We'll starve!" Bouki said.

Malik patted Dru's pocket.

"Oh!" Dru said. She pulled out the coin she had taken from the shipwreck and passed it to Corinne.

"What about this?" Corinne asked.

Kahiri squinted. "Where did you get that?"

"Is it enough to pay for breakfast?"

Kahiri took the coin to his mother. She immediately looked in the direction of the fort, on the other side of the beach. His mother called another vendor over. While they turned the coin in their hands, Kahiri packed the accra and slipped away.

The children dove into the saltfish cakes greedily as Kahiri crawled to the water close to the chattering mermaids.

"Which one of them is Mami Wata?" he asked.

"Who?" Bouki asked, but Malik slapped his hand over his brother's mouth, knocking one of the accra to the ground. Without missing a beat, Bouki swiped it up, blew the dirt off, and popped it back in. He made a face. "Sandy."

Corinne remembered Mami Wata from the wall painting. "Why do you think she is one of them?"

"She's a water goddess, and she can look like anything she wants," Kahiri said. "They are mermaids. One of them must be her."

"I'm Mami Wata," Corinne said quickly, ignoring the looks from her friends. "I am the goddess. And I'm in charge of them."

The boy looked Corinne and the others up and down, then shook his head. "You don't look like a goddess to me."

"You just said I can look like anything," Corinne said. "So why do you doubt me?"

Kahiri grunted. "Because I know girls, and you look just like one of those. Right down to the way you are trying to fool me."

"Being one thing and then another is nothing to me." She pointed to the mermaids. "They were girls too. They lived here once." Corinne called to the mermaids. "This boy might be able to help us."

The mermaids' faces lit up. They talked over each other in that same language the vendors used. Kahiri leaned in, trying to understand all of them at once. Finally, he turned to Corinne and said, "Okay, you are real."

"But are *you* real?" Noyi asked. She pulled closer to Kahiri. When the water became too shallow to swim in, she dragged herself, dark blue tail and all, onto the bank. As soon as she touched dry land, her skin began to change. The soft brown of her upper body turned ashen and then puckered. She was drying out in the sun. The color in her blue tail paled, and the fins went from a sparkling silver to a flat, dull gray.

Malik and Corinne ran and pulled her back into the water. Noyi's skin and scales returned to normal. "Stay where you are," Corinne commanded. "It's not safe for you on land." She turned to Kahiri. "We need your help to find a jewel. It looks like—"

"The bottom of the sea?" Kahiri said. "Everybody knows Mami Wata's—your—stone, and that if you rub it you will have good luck for life. The woman who owns it is the richest person around."

Corinne squared her shoulders and lifted her chin the way she did when she was negotiating. "It's mine and I need it back," she said.

"That won't be easy," said Kahiri. "Ma Dessaly doesn't let anybody see it, and she won't believe you are Mami Wata."

"I will just have to convince her," Corinne said. She unbraided the few remaining plaits so she looked more like the painting of Mami Wata.

Kahiri raised his eyebrows. "You will have to do more than that," he said. "It would help if you used your snakes."

"Snakes!" said Dru.

Kahiri scooped down into a patch of grass and grabbed a writhing little snake with a coppery pattern on its back, a yellow belly, and eyes that looked too large for its thin body. He held it up to Corinne's face. She stumbled back. "Why do you look so sweaty?" Kahiri asked.

"It's hot!" Corinne said. But she felt the accra turning in her stomach, threatening to come up.

Kahiri held the snake out farther so that Corinne had no choice but to take it.

"Owshhh!"

"What did you say?" Corinne asked.

"I didn't say anything," Kahiri said.

"Sssqueeze sssofter, pleassse!"

The only thing that could have been speaking to her was the snake. Corinne loosened her grip on the reptile.

"Thanks," it said.

"What's the matter?" Kahiri asked. "You look like you're going to be sick."

"Spit over so," the little snake said. "Please."

"Better do what it says," said Sisi.

"Better do what who says?" Dru asked.

"The snake," said Sisi. "It asked her not to throw up on it."

"Can you hear it talk?" Dru asked Corinne.

Corinne could only nod. If she tried to speak, she was afraid she really would throw up. She took a deep breath and draped the snake around her neck carefully, trying not to shudder at the feel of its skin—like soft armor—against her own. She remembered the scales Mama D'Leau had put on her tongue and in her ears. Was this what they were for?

Kahiri's face relaxed. "Of course she can hear it," he said. "She's the goddess."

Corinne tried to set her shoulders back, to relax her muscles, but the unsettling feeling in her stomach would not go away.

Kahiri tilted his head and squinted at Corinne. "More snakes would be better."

"Do you have any little friends, snake?" Corinne asked.

"Why do you want us?" it asked.

"Mami Wata always has snakes," she said.

The snake made little wriggling twists as it laughed. "You are certainly not Mami Wata!"

Corinne squeezed the snake again and it stopped laughing.

"I see how it is," it said.

Kahiri looked to where he had found the snake and uncovered a few small eggs in the sand. "Look," he said.

Corinne grabbed one of them. "Yours?" she asked.

"That's a nasty move!" The snake gave her a hard look with its green and black eyes, and Corinne felt her face flush. "It's a snare!" it said, flicking its tongue. When Corinne didn't put back the egg, the snake lowered its head. "How many of my friends do you need?"

"As many as you can bring," Corinne said.

The snake wriggled until Corinne dropped it on the ground. It slithered off in the grass.

"So now she can talk to snakes?" Bouki whispered. "Brother, this jumbie thing really has its benefits, doesn't it?"

Dru took the little egg from Corinne. "You wouldn't have really hurt it, would you?" she asked.

Corinne wanted to say that she would not have. But she had to get the jewel for Mama D'Leau. Her friends' lives were at stake.

21

Try a Thing

The long grass rustled and soft hissing grew louder. Corinne counted eleven snakes undulating along the bank. Her skin prickled, and despite the sun beating down, she shivered. As they got closer, the cacophony of voices hissed about a *dubious rescue* and *enormous bullies* and *unseemly creatures stealing eggs*. As they came out into the open, Corinne squeezed her eyes shut, wondering how so many fangs would feel sinking into her.

"Silence, all of you!" the little snake snapped. The hissing died down. "Well, everyone's present," it said. "You will replace my descendants now?"

"If you help me," Corinne said.

After the snake agreed, Dru and Kahiri carefully put the eggs back. Corinne put the first snake on her shoulders, then one by one she added the others. They flicked their tongues and slithered on her skin. Some got tangled in her loose hair, and others complained about how the buttons on her shirt scraped their scales.

"I changed my mind," Bouki whispered to Malik. "The jumbie thing maybe doesn't have that many benefits."

Malik shrugged and reached out to touch one of the snakes.

Kahiri and the mermaids talked, then he put his lips to the water as if he was getting a drink. Then the mermaids left, dragging themselves over the shallow spit to open water. "I told them it's not safe close to the road," he explained. "They asked me to look for their families, and they told me to put my lips to the water and call for them when I had something to say."

"Let's go," Corinne said.

"What if this doesn't work?" Dru whispered.

"Sometimes you just have to try a thing," Bouki said. He and Malik crested the little hill that separated them from the road.

Corinne was aware of all the people staring at them the moment they were out in the open. Vendors' mouths gaped with surprise or twisted with laughter, while some whispered behind their hands or called out to them loudly. Corinne didn't understand most of what they said, but she didn't need to know their words to understand what they were thinking.

Kahiri ducked to avoid his mother and led them into the village. He walked ahead, seemingly unbothered by the attention, though most of the looks were directed at Corinne and the snakes writhing over her shoulders. As they went, a few people fell into step behind them.

"How will you find out about their families?" Corinne asked, trying to take her mind off the small chattering parade.

"They were taken on a slave ship," he said. "I know that from the coin you gave me. So they lived here centuries ago. And Ababuo remembers that her family herded cattle. It's not much to go on, but I know who to ask."

Corinne rubbed the spot where her own coin was, feeling the edges of it through the fabric of her pocket.

"It would help to know how they came to be mermaids. How did you turn them?"

"That's not important," Corinne said.

"Watch her swerve from the facts!" hissed the first snake. "It was so . . . it was so . . ."

"Obtuse?" suggested another.

"Yes!"

"She's a liar."

"An impersonator!"

"Such a slimy thing to do!"

"Then where have you been all this time?" Kahiri asked.

"I've been . . . I've been . . . there are other people who need my help, you know."

"Ha ha ha! No answer for that either!" a fat snake said, sliding over and under its friends.

"Stop shifting!"

"I'm only searching for some shade!" the snake complained. "It's not nice to be exposed to all of this sun."

Corinne tried, unsuccessfully she was sure, to keep the disgust from her face.

"Some people say no one has seen you for centuries. Some people say they see you all the time," Kahiri continued. They turned down another road and Corinne still didn't offer anything.

Kahiri chewed on his bottom lip, then said, "Some people say you are only a made-up story."

Dru, Bouki, and Malik looked on silently, with concern growing in their eyes. Corinne felt hot and frustrated, and she wanted more than anything to fling the snakes off her neck. She stopped walking, and the little crowd behind them stopped as well. She leveled a steely look at Kahiri and blew breath from her nose like an angry bull. "If you know so much, you know that it's improper to question me."

Kahiri became pale.

"You're lucky I've let you get away with it so far," Corinne said. "But my patience is running out."

Kahiri gulped and moved faster. Then he asked, "Why don't you speak Twi anymore? Your other . . . friends do."

"Maybe I . . . I forgot," she managed to whisper.

"You forgot," Kahiri said loudly.

Murmurs scattered through the crowd. Some sucked their teeth and shook their heads. Most dropped away, but a few children still skipped along.

"Here reminds me of home," Dru said.

The wooden houses with galvanized metal roofs looked very much like the ones on their island, painted in bright colors, surrounded by yards filled with palm and fruit trees. Behind whitewashed open brick walls, children chattered and giggled. But here, the land was all flat. There were no undulating hills, the sweet scent of guava and sugarcane was absent from the air, and the salty smell of the sea could no longer reach them.

"I know why you did it, I think," Kahiri said to Corinne. "Why you turned the girls into mermaids." He whispered the last part so only she could hear.

"Why?" Corinne asked.

"You were lonely," he said. "There is no one like you. You wanted a family."

Corinne wondered if it was every jumbie's habit to take family by force. But why else would Mama D'Leau have turned these four girls into mermaids, leaving others behind?

"Kahiri!" Bouki snapped. "When are we getting there?"

"Now," Kahiri said. He pointed to a large white house at the end of the road.

Corinne became nervous at the thought of convincing Ma Dessaly to give up the stone. The snakes slipped and slapped against her sweaty skin, making her shudder as they hissed complaints in her ears.

"We are sweltering!"

"My skin is shriveled!"

"She is killing us on purpose!"

"She won't. She needs our help with this escapade. But still, watch for deception. She's an egg-stealer, after all."

Kahiri opened the gate to a yard cooled by large fruit trees. He let only Corinne and her friends in, leaving the stragglers to peep through the painted wrought iron or the open brick of the white wall.

The house was larger and fancier than the others they had passed. Corinne had never seen one like it. Everything was white. Its walls gleamed in the sun. There was a lower verandah covered in tile and another one above it. Corinne wondered how many people lived here. A teak tree loomed over the house at one side, and on the other, there were lime and soursop. But most impressive were the masses of bougainvillea that ringed the yard. The paper-thin pale pink and white blossoms shivered in the air. A few blew off the stems, brushing whisper-soft against Corinne's skin. And even the little snakes seemed soothed by the cool calmness of Ma Dessaly's yard.

"Ɛna mema wo aha!" Kahiri called.

A woman wearing all white, from her headscarf to the wide, cotton dress that fell to her ankles, stepped out of the heavy wooden door and onto the tile verandah. She was tall and thick. Her feet slapped the ground and spread wide. Her hands went straight to her hips, making her look even wider and larger. "Hello, hello," she began, and finished her greeting to Kahiri in Twi. But she tilted her head when she saw Corinne, and her greeting trailed off. A look Corinne could not describe came over her face. It didn't feel friendly.

Kahiri bowed his head slightly. "Someone has come looking for you."

Corinne took a step forward.

"What's that shaking?" the little snake asked.

Corinne realized it was the thudding of her heart.

"For me?" Ma Dessaly said, picking up Kahiri's English. "What do you want, little girl?"

"I have come back for the jewel," she said softly.

"Eh?"

Next to Corinne, Dru, Bouki, and Malik were stiff as boards. But Kahiri pushed her forward. "Louder," he whispered.

"The jewel," Corinne said. Her voice seemed to have

squeezed out of a crack, starting small and getting too loud at the end.

Ma Dessaly eyed Corinne as if she was crazy. "What jewel is that?"

Corinne planted her feet wide to match Ma Dessaly's and puffed out her chest. "You know which one," she said. "Bring it to me."

Ma Dessaly's large frame began to shake, and she shook her head. "You . . . you don't look like what I expected," she said. A giggle escaped from her, and she held her hand to her lips.

Corinne tried to be still, but the more she tried, the squirmier she felt. Ma Dessaly wiped a few tears from her eyes and stopped chuckling.

"Ma," Kahiri said. "She really is the goddess."

Ma Dessaly folded her arms. "If I catered to every fool, crazy person, or trickster who came to this house, what position would I be in? Where is your mother, Kahiri? Does she know you came here to harass me?"

"No, Ma," Kahiri said quietly.

The woman looked Corinne up and down. "And if you are Mami Wata, then you should be able to get by me and take what's yours, not so? Go ahead. Try to find it." She planted herself more firmly on the ground and arched one eyebrow to complete the challenge.

Corinne dropped her head.

"It's wrong to impersonate a goddess," Ma Dessaly

said. "Whatever you think you are going to get will turn sour." She shifted her weight to one leg. "Wo din de sɛn? Who are you, really?"

Corinne felt the wind knocked out of her. She didn't know. She stammered something that didn't sound like her name, or a goddess's, or even Mama D'Leau's.

Ma Dessaly took two long steps and grabbed Corinne by the arm. The snakes slid off and one latched on to Ma Dessaly's finger with its fangs. The woman spun and flung the snake clear across the yard.

"Scatter!" the little snake called out.

Ma Dessaly hopped out of the way as snakes slithered around her. She grunted and stamped her feet.

"It's an ambush!" the little snake yelled, and the snakes turned on Ma Dessaly. Her eyes went from fury to fear in an instant. She hopped and screeched like a frightened child. Her size and bulk brought her down hard on the ground. She slipped on the tail of one snake and fell back, crushing a bougainvillea. One of the snakes crawled in after her and she leapt out, screaming, "Stop them!" Her voice was several octaves higher than it had been moments before. "Get them out of my yard!"

Bouki and Malik set off trying to scoop up the snakes, but Dru would only get close enough to push them with her sandaled foot. Corinne didn't help.

"What are you doing?" the little snake hissed. "Isn't this what you wanted? A diversion?"

"Yes, a ruse," another snake said as it darted to a shady spot and let out a long sigh of delight.

Corinne noticed that although her friends were scooping up snakes, they were putting them down again just a few feet away.

Kahiri was standing at the door to the house. "Some got in here!" he yelled, and he waved at Corinne to follow.

Ma Dessaly opened her eyes wide and tiptoed clumsily to the house with the hem of her dress gathered up in her wide palms, screaming, "Ah ah ah!" with each step.

"Go on!" the little snake in the shade called out. "This subterfuge will only last so long. She will see it's a scam and she will slaughter us for sure!"

Corinne nodded and ran into the house after Kahiri. Ma Dessaly ran back out with a long-handled broom gripped over her head like a club. Corinne heard the scrape of the bristles against the stones outside and the crack of the handle amid a string of Ma Dessaly's screams.

The house was a large, open space with few places to hide anything. Ma Dessaly was clearly its sole occupant. Kahiri searched through cupboards. Corinne ran upstairs and looked through a bedroom, digging down into a woven basket of dirty clothes, all white. She tunneled under the bed and climbed up to high shelves but didn't find the stone. She went to another room and saw Ma Dessaly through the window, swatting wildly with the broken broom at the slithering snakes, as Dru and Bouki moved them just out of her way. Malik dug in a corner. He was up to his elbows in red mud. He looked up at Corinne and shook his head. She continued searching but turned up nothing. Kahiri met her at the bottom of the stairs. His hands were empty. The screaming outside had dissipated.

"We have to go," Kahiri said.

Corinne nodded and ran out. She and Kahiri scooped up snakes as they went.

"The escapade is over!" the first snake called. "Retreat!"

"I hope this sorry episode was successful," said a snake hiding in a puddle as Bouki snatched it up.

The five children ran out of the gate with snakes swinging from their hands.

"Scarcely," the little snake said. "It was a disaster."

22

Things Fall Apart

Kahiri led them on a roundabout route down narrow alleyways, and through high grass that made their skin itchy, and murky, ankle-deep water that made their sandals ooze and squish. The moment they were close enough to the inlet where they had all met, the snakes twisted, launched themselves like springs out of the children's hands, and made off, spitting out a litany of insults as they slithered away.

"Gutless!"

"Simpletons!"

"Imbeciles!"

They were far upstream from where they had met Kahiri; here the water ranged from knee- to shoulder-high. As the five of them waded through, the rocks at the bottom bruised their ankles, and their wet clothes and shoes chafed their skin. Kahiri kept opening and closing his mouth as though something was on his mind until Corinne finally snapped, "What?"

"You are not the goddess," he said slowly.

"No," Corinne whispered.

"You are a crook, then. Like all the others who have tried to get Ma Dessaly's stone."

"It's not hers," Dru said. "We didn't lie about that."

Without looking at her, Kahiri said, "It is if the goddess left it to her."

Corinne stopped in a waist-deep spot. "We were sent to get it," she said. "From across the sea. The mermaids brought us. They're her mermaids. Not ours. We didn't even know about them before yesterday. But it's not Ma Dessaly's stone. And if we don't get it back, people are going to be hurt."

"People here will be hurt if you take it," Kahiri said.

Corinne shook her head. "Children have been taken. Mama . . . Mami Wata won't help us find them unless we bring the stone back."

"That doesn't sound like the goddess," Kahiri said.

"People change," Bouki said drily. "Even goddesses."

"How?" Kahiri asked.

Corinne took a breath. She told him about Severine, the white witch, the night on the cliff, the orange trees she planted, the earthquake, the missing children, and Mama D'Leau.

"I don't know if it's the same goddess," Kahiri said. "Mami Wata is helpful. Your Mama D'Leau doesn't sound very nice."

"How else would she know about the stone?" Dru asked.

"Many people have heard about the stone," Kahiri said. "Many people have done all kinds of things to try to get it."

"People who can command mermaids?" Corinne asked.

Kahiri looked like he was working a thought on his tongue, rolling it around and tasting it. But finally he swallowed and said nothing.

"You believe us, don't you?" Dru asked.

"I will try to find out about the mermaids' families," Kahiri said. "But I can't help anymore with the stone. You will have to figure that out on your own."

Corinne collapsed on the soft, silty ground and took off her sandals so she could wash her feet and her shoes could dry out. Everyone else did the same.

"Terrific," Bouki said. "How are we going to do that?"

Corinne lay back with her hair spread out around her and squinted up at the sun. "No idea," she said.

"Whatever you do, you can't do it here," Kahiri said. "Ma Dessaly is here. And she is angrier than I've ever seen her."

All five of them scrambled to the top of the bank and watched the commotion on the street. Ma Dessaly and Kahiri's mother were in a heated argument, and they had attracted a crowd.

"She's looking for you," Kahiri said.

Bouki turned to Corinne. "What now, goddess?"

"If she's here, it means that she isn't at the house to stop us," Corinne said.

"We already looked there," Kahiri said. "She probably has the place locked up tight."

"If we only had a little more time, we could search properly," Corinne said.

Dru shook her head. "It's not right. Even if the stone isn't hers, it's not right to break into someone's house and go through their things." She paused. "I mean, a second time."

"But if we don't, what will happen to Laurent? Or Marlene?" Corinne asked.

While they argued over what to do, Malik pulled at Corinne's clothes, and poked her in the arm, and waved his hands in front of her face.

"What, Malik?" Corinne yelled. "Sometimes I wish you would just talk. You can do it. I've heard you."

Malik froze, and the excitement drained from his face. Dru and Bouki pulled him closer. Corinne knew she should say she was sorry, but she clenched her jaw tight and scanned the crowd again.

"It's time for me to go," Kahiri said. "I'll go up the river so they won't look for you here, but it's not safe. You'll have to find somewhere else to hide."

"Where?" Dru asked.

Kahiri pointed to the large sand-colored fort. "Go to the castle," he said. "There are plenty of rooms to hide in, and nobody stays there after dark."

"How long is it going to take for you to find out about the mermaids' families?" Dru asked.

Kahiri shrugged. "They've been gone a long, long time." He walked away.

"You three go to the castle and wait," Corinne said.

"You're not doing this alone," said Dru. "We came too. Because of you." Her words were sharp, but she looked down at the ground when she said them.

"What if they've already been found?" Bouki said. "What if all of this is for nothing?"

"And what if they haven't?" Dru argued. "If we go back empty-handed, it really will have been for nothing."

Corinne shook her head. "A jumbie wouldn't give them up so easily," she said.

"What does Mama D'Leau want with them anyway?" Dru asked. "She has the mermaids." She picked at the ends of her hair, frowned at the strands in her fingers, then tucked them behind her ears.

"Why do you think it's her?" Corinne asked.

"Who else would it be?" Bouki argued.

"You're defending a jumbie?" asked Dru.

Corinne folded her arms across her chest. "What's wrong with defending a jumbie? I'm one."

"Well, not exactly," Dru said. "You're—"

"A jumbie," Corinne said flatly. "Just like Mama D'Leau. Just like Severine."

"Don't say *her* name," Bouki said with a shudder. "She's gone. She doesn't matter anymore."

"Maybe she does," Corinne said.

"We all know it was a water jumbie who was taking the children," Bouki said. "They all went missing by the water. You heard one of them sing. What kind of jumbies sing, Corinne? I bet this whole thing is a game for Mama D'Leau. Maybe Laurent and the others are in some other part of the world too. This could be how she has her fun, Corinne. Does that sound like a jumbie thing to do?"

There was a sharpness in Bouki's jaw and an arch in his eyebrows that unsettled Corinne. Her friends had never looked at her this way before.

"It's very strange," Dru said.

"Everything jumbies do is strange. Seeing in the dark, talking to snakes!" Bouki gestured wildly and Corinne's hands closed into fists. The next moment, Corinne had been knocked back. Both Corinne and Bouki fell in the sand and slid down the bank. Malik stood over both of them. His head was lowered, and his chest heaved. He drew a finger up slowly and pressed it to his lips. Then he pointed toward the vendors.

Corinne and Bouki crawled up to see what he was pointing at. Kahiri was there, getting yelled at by his mother, while Ma Dessaly stood over him, making him shrink like a wilting plant. As soon as Kahiri stopped talking, Ma Dessaly motioned with her thick arms, and two men joined her. She pointed in different directions and the men moved off, looking into and under stalls, behind crates, and up into trees.

"A search party," Corinne said.

Without another word, they returned to the water and made a quick route back to the sea. In minutes, they were in deep enough water to dive under the waves and swim for the castle. They resurfaced only for sips of air until they came to a jetty of slippery rocks that led to a series of broken, weather-worn, splintery stairs on the other side of the beach. Above them was the castle.

23

Two Stories

Kahiri wiped the tears from his eyes and the snot from his nose as he walked the curving road to Manu's house. His mother had been angry. He slipped away, knowing it would make her even angrier, but he had made a promise, and he was going to try to keep it. He flipped Dru's coin into the air, once, twice. It fell on his palm with a light tap. It was heavier than a fifty-pesewas coin, but about the same size. This coin was from another time, and only Manu still told stories that stretched so far back.

He came to a small house with faded green paint. He pushed open the wobbly gate and went up to the verandah, where an old man sat in a rocking chair carving a small figure.

"Mema wo aha, Kahiri!" the man said.

"Agya mema wo aha," Kahiri said. He sat on the floor in front of the rocking chair and watched Manu dig the tip of the knife into the wood with quick twists. When he stopped and blew off the dust, he had carved one eye on the little figure. He turned it to Kahiri.

"What can I do for you?" Manu asked in soft Twi.

Kahiri flipped the coin to Manu. "I will tell you a story," he said. "And then you will tell me one."

Manu squinted at the coin, and then at Kahiri. "All right," he said. "Begin."

24

In a Fine Castle

Corinne pulled everyone under the broken stairs and looked through the cracks as Ma Dessaly and the two men searched all three levels of the castle. They hung on to thick posts as they waited.

"He told on us," Bouki said. "How would they know to look here?"

"There's nowhere else to hide," Corinne said.

"We can't stay in the water," Dru added.

Malik pointed to a seawall against the castle that was broken in one spot, like a chipped tooth. The crack was low enough for them to pull themselves over. He took a gulp of air and swam the entire length to the wall, resurfacing just as Ma Dessaly arrived and looked out at the water. If she looked straight down, she would see him. Corinne ducked behind the posts with the others, but she felt as if someone was squeezing her heart in a vise. A few moments later, Ma Dessaly motioned to the men in another part of the castle, and she moved on. Malik flashed his smile across the waves and gave a thumbs-up.

Corinne, Bouki, and Dru met him at the wall. They waited until they could no longer hear the crunch of footsteps before they pulled themselves through the crack.

The castle was a mottled combination of dirty white paint and sandy-colored patches where the paint had peeled off, revealing the raw, crumbling stone underneath. Lines of mold and rot expanded cracks and colored some surfaces shades of poisonous-looking black and green. The walls, the floors, the ceiling—everything was solid, as if the castle had been carved from one boulder. And every level of the castle had a terrace that overlooked the water, where dozens of black cannons peered over the sea like the eyes of an all-seeing monster.

There was a nearby alcove partly filled with heavy black cannon balls. The four of them jammed inside, trying to keep out of sight. But it was not long before their backs ached and their muscles felt stiff. Someone's stomach growled and Corinne's muscles tightened.

"Stop breathing on me," Bouki complained.

"What would you like me to do?" Corinne whispered. "Hold my breath?"

"Try it. Maybe some of that jumbie stuff will kick in."

Corinne pinched what she thought was Bouki's arm, but Dru yelped.

"Sorry," Corinne said.

"Maybe you should say that to Malik," Dru retorted.

"Shh!" Malik said.

Dru moved a leg, and they all tumbled out of the space and then scrambled back. "We can't stay here all day," she whined.

"You all should go back to the mermaids," Corinne said. "I will talk to Ma Dessaly alone."

Bouki rolled his eyes. "This again."

"You don't want to be around a jumbie, so go," Corinne said. "Nobody is keeping you here."

"But you brought us," Bouki said. "We wouldn't be here if you hadn't thought of us. And why did you, anyway?"

Corinne bit her lip. "Because I couldn't do it without you," she said. "I knew I couldn't."

Bouki looked genuinely sorry. Dru gave Corinne a sideways smile and Malik winked.

"Anyway, Dru's right," Corinne said. "We can't stay here."

"Well, we got dragged across the whole ocean," Bouki said. "So you're not doing anything alone."

Malik ventured onto the landing. He stayed low until he reached a set of stairs. He called his friends over with one finger. Beyond them was an open courtyard. There were stairs on both sides. Facing the sea side were the cannons, each with a pyramid of stacked cannon balls, and at the back were rooms with peeling, faded blue doors. Ma Dessaly and the two men were already searching the next level up.

Malik dashed across the courtyard and pulled at one of the doors. A large iron latch stuck on the clasp, so he had to pull a few times to get it open. The door screeched on its hinges. He cringed and opened it just wide enough for everyone to squeeze through.

From a crack in the door, they saw Ma Dessaly appear on one set of stairs and the two men on the other. They searched down into the courtyard. Malik tapped Corinne on the shoulder and made a motion across his chest with his hand. Bouki chuckled.

"What is it?" Dru whispered.

"She has the stone on her. Look," Corinne said.

Ma Dessaly was wearing the same white dress from before, but there was a bag hung across her chest from her shoulder to her hip. Inside was something lumpish and heavy-looking. Ma Dessaly kept one hand firmly on the strap as she called instructions to the two men.

"Do you really think . . ." Dru began.

"What better way to keep it safe than to have it on you

where you can be sure no one will take it," Bouki said. He turned to Corinne and pointed at her necklace. "Isn't that where you keep your most prized possession? Where you can touch it?"

Dru sighed. "That means it's going to be even harder to get."

"This is when it's helpful to know a couple of thieves," said Bouki. Malik rubbed his palms together, and Bouki stretched his fingers. "This is going to be difficult, brother," he said. "But not impossible."

Malik screwed up his lips.

"Well, maybe it will be very close to impossible, but there is a sliver of hope."

Malik arched an eyebrow.

"A very, very, very thin sliver."

"So what's the plan?" Dru asked.

"You approve of thieving now?" Bouki asked, smiling.

"This is different," Dru said. "We have to get the stone, otherwise—"

"Right, right, the missing children. But we are also children, and there are more of us than there are ones missing back home." Malik jabbed Bouki with an elbow. "Uh, that we know of. And it would be simpler to cut our losses and go."

"But then you wouldn't get to show us your excellent thieving skills," Corinne pointed out.

"True," Bouki said. He lifted his chin and smirked.

Malik and Bouki went to work in a corner of the room covered in a thin layer of sand that had blown in from the beach. They drew up a first draft of their plan, wiped it away, and drew again.

The room was dark, except for slivers of light that came in through windows too high to see out of. There were no glass panes, so sand from the beach had settled in thin, uneven layers that crunched under their feet. Against the walls were long dark stains, taller than Corinne. In a few places there were etched markings that looked like someone had made them with the sharp edge of a stone, but she didn't know what they said. Some of the etchings were only a series of straight lines. Those, Corinne understood. Whoever had made them was counting. In one spot, there were thirty-three. *What were they counting?* she wondered. People? Meals? Days? Weeks? She saw a length of chain in one corner, and the memory of the chains on the ship came straight at her like an arrow. The chain was heavy, almost too heavy for her to pick up, but she did, feeling the weight against her hand.

"Were the mermaids here?" Dru asked.

"They were girls once," Corinne said. "And they were chained on that ship. Maybe they were here first." Corinne's stomach soured, and her throat tightened.

"What is this place?" Dru asked.

25

Hide and Thief

Kahiri had called it the castle, but it didn't look like a place for kings or queens. If each of the rooms on this floor had the same high windows, they probably also had the same chains, and maybe even the same etched tally marks. Castle seemed like too soft a word for a place where everything looked heavy and dangerous.

Corinne was pulled from her thoughts by the sharp snap of Bouki's fingers. "That's it, brother," he said. "Brilliant." He rubbed Malik's curly hair. Then he turned to the girls. "It's going to take all of us. Your speed, Dru, and your climbing skills, Corinne. We're going to make them split up and leave Ma Dessaly by herself. She doesn't think we can get the stone from her if she can feel it all the time on her body." He grinned. "She's so sure that it will almost be too easy to take."

"How?" Corinne asked.

"Never ask a master his secrets," Bouki said. "All you have to do is not get caught." Bouki brought them to the drawing he and Malik had made in the sand and explained. When he was finished, Malik bolted from the room. He opened another door all the way, letting it creak loud and long. Just as Bouki had predicted, Ma Dessaly and the two men came to investigate. One of the men came with Ma Dessaly down the staircase nearest to the children and the other ran to the stairs on the other side of the courtyard. They were going to surround them. Corinne came out of the room and climbed the wall, putting her feet into the cracks until she reached the window slits and then pushing herself up to the next level, where Ma Dessaly and the men had been moments before. There, she picked up a handful of gravel and tossed it at Ma Dessaly and each of the men, to distract them long enough for Dru and Bouki to run off in different directions. Corinne gaped so long at Dru's speed that she didn't notice one of the men running toward her until he was at the top of the stairs. She tossed the rest of the stones at him. He skidded and grabbed the railing to keep from falling, giving Corinne time to slip inside an open room and hide beneath an old wooden desk. She heard the scrape of the man's shoes on the sand-covered floor and his hard, gasping breath as he looked into the room, but he moved on quickly. As soon as she was sure he was gone, Corinne got up to look around.

Unlike on the level below, the windows here were low enough for anyone to see into or out of. Corinne closed the broken shutters, blotting out the sun except for a few shards of light. There was no other furniture besides the heavy desk. Corinne traced her finger over the top. There was a round hole on the right and a smooth groove, just deep enough to fit her finger, running nearly the full width of the desk. Corinne pulled the desk's drawers. They stuck, but she rocked them open. Her father often oiled the wooden surfaces in their house to make sure that they didn't bow and bend with age and exposure to the damp sea air. No one had been taking care of the furniture here. The drawers were musty and empty.

Corinne listened for footsteps and moved to another room where she found a large bed frame, a stool, a smaller desk, and a peeling leather trunk. She looked inside the trunk and found a torn, yellowed cloth with the remnants of a pattern that reminded her of the vendors' clothes. Blocky pyramids lay on a background of stripes of varying widths. She felt the paperiness of it between her fingers and smelled it. It had a sweet scent like faded perfume. It was still in her hands when Ma

Dessaly walked in, taking up nearly the entire doorway, blocking out what little light there was.

"Where are your snakes now?" she bellowed.

• • •

Ma Dessaly sneered at Corinne as the two men dragged her friends into the room. Ma Dessaly barked an order and the men stood outside the door, like guards.

"My boys," Ma Dessaly said. "They are good boys. They always do what I ask them to." Beads of sweat glistened on her dark face. She shifted the strap of the bag with her thumb. There was a dark red imprint where the thin fabric had dug down into her flesh.

"I want to know where you come from," Ma Dessaly asked. "How do you know about Mami Wata and the opal when you don't speak the language, and you are not dressed like anyone here?" She used a handkerchief to wipe her forehead. "Well?"

"What is this place?" Corinne asked.

"I am asking the questions, miss."

"Kahiri said this was a castle, but it doesn't look like a castle."

Ma Dessaly lowered onto the stool. It creaked under her. "All right. Yes. The people who built this place called it the castle."

"But it's a prison," Bouki said.

"Not exactly," Ma Dessaly said. Her bulk had somehow changed. She seemed softer, as though her muscles and bones had all relaxed. Her head drooped. "The people who built this weren't from here. They came to capture people and then they put them on ships to be sold across the ocean as slaves."

Corinne felt the surroundings closing in, as if everything and everyone in it had become tighter.

"But not everyone survived the trip," Dru said.

"True."

"We saw one of the ships," Corinne said. "It wasn't that far out from here. There were chains on it like the ones we saw in the rooms downstairs." She stepped forward. "There was this." She pulled out the coin from the wreckage.

Ma Dessaly perked up. She held the coin to a shaft of sunlight. She waved for the children to come closer. "You see here?" She pointed at the image etched into the coin. "Two doves, with the ocean in the middle. That's for loved ones on either side of the water. But it's not a coin." She flipped it to the underside, which was blank. "There would have been a handle here. It's a seal. Used to close letters. Tell me how you found it."

Corinne didn't know if she could trust Ma Dessaly. But Ma Dessaly had no reason to trust Corinne, either. She had introduced herself with a lie. Maybe it was time to tell the truth. "Four mermaids brought us across the ocean to get the stone from you."

Corinne felt Ma Dessaly's muscles vibrate like a pulled

string. She looked at Corinne intently and her hand slid down to the stone in her bag.

"Here," Dru said. She put a large greenish fish scale into Ma Dessaly's hand. One of Ellie's.

Ma Dessaly examined the scale like she did the coin. "You have seen Mami Wata, then?" she asked.

Corinne shifted from one foot to the other. She wasn't exactly sure whether Mama D'Leau and Mami Wata were the same. "She sent us for that," she said, pointing at the bag. Corinne figured if she didn't specify which *she* she meant, whatever Ma Dessaly assumed was not her fault.

Ma Dessaly plucked the stone from the bag. It was perfectly round and gleamed in the reddish light of the setting sun. Corinne clutched her mama's stone against her heart.

"It looks like someone scooped out a piece of the sea," Dru said.

The opal was clear at the surface, but it looked like waving seaweed and colorful pieces of coral had been trapped in the middle. Corinne reached out to touch the jewel, expecting her finger to go through it, like it was a large drop of water, but it was solid. Ma Dessaly turned the stone in her hand, making the shapes in the middle look like they were swaying in a gentle tide.

"Why did she send you?" Ma Dessaly asked.

Corinne told her about the missing children and the favor they had to perform. She didn't mention how terrifying Mama D'Leau was or how she had given them no choice, and no warning. She made it seem like Mama D'Leau was kind, more like Mami Wata might have been. "So you believe us now?" Corinne asked.

Ma Dessaly stood up. "I believe you."

Corinne let out a breath that she didn't know she had been holding in. She put her palm up, waiting for Ma Dessaly to drop the stone into it.

But Ma Dessaly moved to the door. "Come," she said.

The children and the men followed her down to the lowest level of the castle. They faced the water and watched as the sun dove toward it like a red ball. It cast a bloody light over the walls, the cannons, and the ammunition. Behind them were the rooms with the chains.

"Mami Wata saved those girls," Ma Dessaly said. "And she saved my family, too. The opal has been with us for eight generations," she said. "It was the last time anyone saw Mami Wata walking on this shore. Maybe right after that, she took those girls across the ocean with her and left this behind." Ma Dessaly hefted the stone in her hand. "She gave it to my ancestor and told her to keep it with her always. It was a gift, she said, that would keep her family safe, and she was right. It did. But only our family. We were safe while others weren't. Families were torn apart, split across the ocean. But our family was protected and people hated us for it. They said my ancestors should have tried to save others. They called them cruel, and worse things, too. When Mami Wata gave this to us, it was a blessing and a burden." Ma Dessaly nodded, and her sons came up behind the children and opened a grate in the floor of the courtyard. Ma Dessaly's fingers closed over the stone as if they might crush it to dust. "I'm not giving it to you," she said.

"But our friends!" Dru said.

"What about us here?" Ma Dessaly said. "Mami Wata left the stone so my family would be safe from harm and so we would be prosperous. She left it so we would never have to fear losing our loved ones to this place or watch them cross the ocean, never to return. For generations we have been doing well, and this evil place has had no use. Why would I give it up now for some children? How many children do you imagine were already lost across the water?"

"It's not yours to keep," Corinne said. "She wants it back."

Ma Dessaly laughed. She dropped the jewel into the bag and readjusted the strap against her shoulder. Bouki and Malik rushed at her. She swatted them away, but Malik kept pulling at the bag as Bouki tried to defend his brother. Her sons picked them off their mother like fruit off a tree.

"You can't do this," Corinne said. "We came all this way."

Ma Dessaly's sons grabbed her and Dru as well and shoved all four of them into the room beneath the courtyard and closed the iron grate on top of it. The children bounced down the stairs and landed in darkness. Corinne immediately ran back up the steps and pushed against the metal grid. It didn't budge. Ma Dessaly fixed her head tie and smoothed her dress, then she walked grandly out of the castle. She never even looked back.

26

The Door of No Return

All four of them pushing together only got the grating to budge slightly. After several frustrating minutes, they sat on the bottom step and listened to the waves crash against the castle walls. The room was so dark that Corinne couldn't see its sides, and she felt the shadows close in on her like the water in the mermaids' memory. Corinne rushed up the stairs and pushed the grating again. It felt like it was pushing back, as if the steel itself wanted her to fail. She began to cry.

Dru circled her arms around Corinne's waist and dropped her head on Corinne's shoulder.

"Corinne?" Kahiri's voice called out.

"Here!" she called back. She wiped her nose with the back of her hand.

Kahiri's head appeared at the top of the stairs where Ma Dessaly had exited. He ran over to them and knelt above the iron grate. "Are you all right? I saw Ma Dessaly walking away from the castle with a big, big smile on her face. I have never seen her smile like that." He pulled up on the grating while the rest of them pushed from below, and finally, they shoved it all the way open.

The four of them scrambled out.

"What was that place?" Corinne asked.

"They punished people by putting them in that dungeon before they were forced onto slave ships." He pointed at the rooms with the high slit windows toward the back of the courtyard. "Those held the ones who were frightened enough to stay quiet. But you're out now, and you'll be going home soon."

"Without the stone," Corinne muttered.

"How many stones do we need?" Bouki asked, his eyes twinkling.

"Bouki?" Corinne said.

"Corinne?" Bouki answered. He reached into his pocket and pulled out the stone. It took up his entire hand, but there it was, shining like a giant drop of water.

"How did you do it?" Corinne asked.

"Misdirection," Bouki said. He tossed the stone into the air. It came down heavy and his wrist bent under the weight of it. He made a pained face and passed it to his other hand. "While she was trying to fend off Malik, I pulled the stone out of her bag and replaced it with another one."

"She'll figure it out," Kahiri said.

"Not for a while," Bouki said. "She's sure that nothing happened to it. She put it in the bag herself. She's probably not going to check until she gets back home because she won't want anybody else to see it."

"Brilliant," Corinne said.

"I know," he said. "Hey, you didn't bring any more of those saltfish cakes, did you?" He grinned at Kahiri.

Kahiri shook his head. "May I touch it?"

Bouki handed it to him, and Kahiri turned it in his hands, staring with his mouth hanging open. "It's pretty."

"And if it works the way it's supposed to, now you're lucky," Dru said.

Kahiri grinned. He led them toward water. "Time for you to go."

Malik shook his head and pointed toward the sea.

"The mermaids," Dru translated for Kahiri. "You were supposed to find out about their families."

"I have a story," Kahiri said. "Only I'm not sure if it's really about one of them."

Kahiri kept walking toward an open stone doorway that looked out at the sea. The sun had gone down, and the rising moonlight lit his face and the waves in the distance. "Your mermaids, when they were people, would have come through here," he said. "Then they were taken down to the ships. This was the last view they had of home. When you go through these doors, you never return."

They stood in the doorway, silent. Corinne thought about what it would have been like to be forced away from her home, from her family, to an unknown destination, knowing she would never return. Her heart ached and she reached for the stone that hung around her neck, even though her home and her papa waited on the other side of the world and she knew she would return to them. Bouki reached for Malik's fingers and held them tightly.

"But they did return," Dru said. "They are home now."

Kahiri smiled. "Yes. Terrible people stole them away from here. And terrible events brought them back. But after all that time, here they are again." He led them through the door of no return. They climbed down the rickety stairs to the rocky jetty. Corinne put her lips to the salty water and called the mermaids, but they didn't come.

"Try again," Bouki said.

"Sisi would have come if she heard us," Corinne said. "Maybe something is wrong."

"You have to say Boahinmaa," Bouki said.

"That's actually correct," said Dru.

"Don't look so surprised," Bouki said. He narrowed his eyes at her, but smiled.

"They promised to come for me," Kahiri said. He and Corinne put their lips to the waves and called the mermaids' true names, Boahinmaa, Ozigbodi, Gzifa, and Ababuo. A moment later, the mermaids appeared in the water near them.

"Look what we found in a river," Sisi said. The mermaids heaped oysters on the rocks. "There were masses of them."

Bouki knelt gently and wiped a grateful tear from his eyes. Then he picked up a stone and cracked the oysters open by knocking them on their thin edges.

"You can't!" Kahiri protested. "It's bad luck to eat those!" But Bouki was already prying them open and passing them around. Corinne, Dru, Malik, and Bouki fell on the oysters, slurping them out of the shells as Kahiri looked on with worry in his eyes. "Everything will be ruined!" he insisted.

Malik pointed at the jewel in Kahiri's hand.

"We have all the luck we need," Dru said, taking the opal from him.

Malik patted Kahiri sympathetically on the shoulder as he slurped another oyster. Kahiri went to the edge of the rocky jetty and dangled his feet in the water.

"What did you find out about our families?" Noyi asked. She swam to the rocks and held on just beneath Kahiri's knees.

"There was a story about a girl named Boahinmaa, but I don't know if it's you," he said to Sisi.

She swam close. "Tell us."

Ellie and Addie also nestled close to Kahiri against the rocks and listened.

"Boahinmaa was only thirteen when she was stolen in a raid on another village. Her family had traveled, herding their cattle, and she and her youngest brother stayed behind. The brother followed the warriors into the bush, trying to get her back. But he was small, and he didn't have any weapons. So he tracked their footprints and their sounds. When they stopped to rest, he stopped too, but he slept too long and too hard, and when he woke up again, they had moved on.

"The boy wandered the forest for a while, listening and looking for the footprints of the warriors. He found a piece of cloth on a thorn that looked like his sister's skirt. He followed it, and he found another piece and another piece. It led him to where the men were, but by then, it was too late. He was at the outskirts of the warriors' village, and he could not go inside without being seen. The boy waited for days, eating what little he could find in the bush and drinking from streams he had passed, but he never saw his sister again. He returned home with the pieces of her clothes and gave one each to his mother and father and their sisters and brothers as a memory."

Kahiri pulled out a piece of cloth. It was aged and faded, but there was a distinct yellow background with orange lines. "I got this from the man who told me that story," he said.

Sisi had pulled up close. Her uneven tail flipped behind her, dark yellow with red at the tips that looked like frayed cloth.

"Was it you?" Ellie asked.

"I don't remember," Sisi said.

"Why don't we remember everything?" Ellie asked. "Why can't we know about our families when we are so close to home?"

"I'm sorry," Kahiri said. "If I had more time . . ."

"We will come back," Sisi promised. "Merekɔ aba."

Addie removed two of her scales and placed them on Kahiri's ears. "Put your ear to the water and listen."

Kahiri did as he was told while Addie whispered into the water. He stood up beaming. "I heard you!" he said. "How often should I listen to the sea?"

Addie laughed. "Our songs have a way of rippling on the water. Come any time and you will hear them. We will sing to tell you when we can return."

Kahiri looked toward the village with a sad face. "I have to go home," he said. He put his hands in Addie's and they touched their foreheads to each other. "Safe journey. Wo ne nyame nkɔ."

Kahiri picked his way over the rocks to the beach. He walked away, turning back often to watch them until he disappeared beyond the dunes.

• • •

Once the oysters had been devoured, the children care-fully made their way down the side of the stone jetty to the water. Corinne reached a hand out to Sisi, but Sisi didn't take it. The mermaids had gathered close together, watching the path Kahiri had taken home.

"I can't leave without finding my family," Ellie said. "I am home now. Why should I go?"

"I would want to be home too," Corinne said. "But our friends need us. Besides, Kahiri didn't find your fami-lies yet."

Ellie began to cry. "But I am so close to them. I can feel it." She sobbed in the water, making little waves that crashed against the rocks.

"We will come back again," Sisi said. "Just think, maybe by the time we return, Kahiri will be able to tell us about the children of our brothers and sisters."

Ellie shook her head violently. Her braids launched water that caught the moonlight in fast-moving arcs.

"Why can they have their families when we can't have ours?" Ellie shouted. "Why should I leave them behind again? I had no choice before, but I have a choice now."

Ellie sped for land. Corinne reached out to grab her as she had grabbed Noyi that morning, but Ellie slipped between her fingers and Corinne fell into the water. Her heart pounded as she watched the mermaid beach herself. "No!" Corinne called out, but Ellie kept moving across the land. "Do something!" Corinne pleaded with the other mermaids as she swam to Ellie. Noyi dashed forward, but stopped when the water was at her waist. With every moment, Ellie changed. First her skin turned from dark brown to gray, getting paler by the moment, like moth wings. Then the strands of hair in her braids faded to white.

Malik dove into the water. He met Corinne on the beach and they took Ellie's hands and tried to pull her back. Her fingers were brittle as glass and they cracked in their grip. Malik moved to scoop up the mermaid's body. Corinne followed his lead. They tried to drag her back as her bright scales began to shrivel, becoming as delicate as tissue paper. The line down the middle of her tail darkened and sank inward, separating into two legs. Corinne and Malik tried to move more gently as Ellie's entire body faded to the color of beach sand. The breeze peeled the surface of her skin like petals on the wind.

"Ababuo!" the other three mermaids sobbed.

"Slower, Malik!" Corinne said. "We have to be careful."

"Faster!" Bouki shouted. He was looking past Corinne and Malik. Ma Dessaly was running down the sand dunes toward them with her white dress flapping in the wind, her two sons right behind her.

Ellie's body was crumbling in their hands as Ma Dessaly and her sons were getting closer.

"Come on!" Bouki yelled. He grabbed the stone from Dru and dropped it in his pocket, where it bulged against his leg. "There's no time!"

Corinne and Malik looked at each other. They were moving as quickly as they dared, but Ellie was still coming apart. Pieces of her fell to the beach and crumbled into the sand. Malik shook his head and stopped.

"Brother!" Bouki yelled.

"I'm not going without Ellie," Corinne said. "We can't leave her." When they reached the water, they placed what remained of Ellie into the waves. The mermaid's body dissolved like sugar, leaving only a few blue and gold scales in their hands. Corinne fell to her knees and gripped them in her palm.

Malik pulled Corinne's shirt.

Corinne heard the footsteps getting close.

"Stop!" Ma Dessaly screamed.

Anger seared Corinne's heart. "You see?" she said to the other mermaids. "Mama D'Leau will not let you stay here. And if you don't return to her, you know that there is nowhere in the water to hide."

Malik pushed Corinne ahead as the men splashed into the waves behind them. A wave hit Corinne and washed the few glittering remains of Ellie's scales to shore. Malik and Corinne ducked under the water as Dru dove from the jetty. Noyi scooped Dru and Malik under each of her arms, as Addie took Bouki and Corinne clasped hands with Sisi. The men swam into the surf behind them. Sisi slapped one of them with her tail. The other one stopped swimming and opened his mouth in surprise. He put his hand to his throat and surfaced, coughing up water.

Ma Dessaly ran into the waves after them, screaming against the breeze. Corinne looked back as Ma Dessaly's eyes widened at the sight of the mermaids. She picked something out of the water. It sparkled in her hand. She sank to her knees with her hands clasped against her chest, and her eyes raised. Ma Dessaly cried out over the waves, "Forgive me!"

27

Faded Memories

The mermaids moved quickly through the midnight-blue ocean, staying near the surface, where they could see the stars shining down from the sky and occasional flashes of light illuminating the sea beneath them. Even though Corinne's vision had lit up once again, at times she could not tell which way was sea or sky. The mermaids slowed when they approached the broken ship only long enough to exchange silent glances. Corinne was grateful they did not want to linger. Mama D'Leau's pale blue current curved ahead. As soon as they entered it, the mermaids began to chatter.

You're in a better mood, Dru said.

Why wouldn't we be? Noyi asked. *We're heading home after a long swim, even if these two heavy fish don't make it any easier.*

But you said Ghana was your home, Ozigbodi, Corinne said.

What did you call her? Sisi asked.

Ozigbodi.

Sisi giggled. *They don't remember our names!*

Of course not, Noyi said. *They only care about getting a ride. What if I dropped them here in the middle of the sea?*

For something to eat them up? Addie added, giggling.

You wouldn't, Gzifa, Bouki said.

But what are these strange names? Addie asked. *Is it a game? Are you playing with us?*

Don't you remember Ababuo? Corinne asked. *Or Kahiri?*

If this is a game, said Noyi, *it's terrible. We don't know the rules and it seems very cruel to call us names.*

We can be cruel too, Addie said, eyeing Bouki and letting him slip out of her hold. Malik reached for his brother, but Addie quickly grabbed him up again.

Sisi said, *I was your friend. I helped you. Your grand-père—*

I know. I'm sorry, Corinne said. *It's just—*

But before she could explain, the mermaids began to sing. Corinne forgot what she was going to say. Bouki looked at her as she drifted off to sleep, and she thought she heard him say, *Misdirection.*

• • •

Corinne felt something brush against her side, and she opened her eyes. It was the sargassum they had passed on the night they left the island. Corinne lifted her hand out of the water and the tiny sargassum leaves tickled her fingers. Small, flat-bodied fish darted out of the plants. Corinne grabbed a handful of sargassum and passed it to Sisi, who popped it in her mouth.

The seafloor rose, and Corinne's friends began to wake. Beds of coral appeared in the distance and colorful fish, crabs, and shrimp darted out as the group drew near. Malik waved his hand at a blue-green fish, and when it came close, he traced his finger over its body. Dru shrank back against Noyi, but her eyes roved, watching everything that darted by.

Where are all the fishermen? Bouki asked. *All the fish are here, waiting to be caught.*

The water was beginning to brighten, so Corinne guessed it was close to sunrise. The fishermen always started before dawn, but the surface of the sea was empty. A school of flying fish dove under them and then shot back up, breaching the water. They spread their silvery wings and glided in the air. One of them hovered low and its tail made a long zigzagging line in the water.

Bouki reached away from Addie, trying to touch it, but Addie pulled him back hard. *Aren't any of you hungry? What if there is nothing to eat when we get home?* he asked.

Bouki, you live in a bakery, Dru said.

You can never be too sure of anything. At least let me try *to catch one.*

Addie let him drop beneath her as the flying fish dove again, but she kept a tight hold on his hand. He came up empty.

Shouldn't we be there by now? Dru asked.

You will be there soon enough, Noyi snapped.

The flying fish continued in bounding arcs ahead of them, almost like they were escorting them home. Past the gardens of coral, Corinne broke the surface, anxious to see the island. She shook water out of her ears, and the dull silence was immediately replaced with a loud crackling noise and a series of pops. This wasn't the sound of the sea. There was an acrid scent in the air.

"Fire!" she cried. "The island is on fire!"

The mermaids rose above the waves and watched as black smoke spiraled into the sky. White ash fell on their faces and in their hair. Some of it dissolved, and some marked them with white streaks that reminded Corinne of Ellie's final moments.

"Take us straight home," Corinne pleaded.

Sisi shook her head. "Mama D'Leau will want you right away."

"Our home is burning!" Dru shouted. "When you found your home across the ocean, you didn't want to leave it. We could barely tear you away."

"This is our home," Sisi said calmly. "Are you playing

that game again? Because I don't understand it." She pulled Corinne roughly underwater. The other two mermaids followed.

They found Mama D'Leau floating over the broken and bleached remains of a coral reef, which looked pale and eerie, like a ghost under the water. Mama D'Leau fussed over it like a mother might with a sick child.

Our home is on fire, Corinne said before Mama D'Leau even had a chance to look up. *We have to get back.*

What can the four of you little fish do? Noyi asked.

Mama D'Leau raised an eyebrow, and Noyi bit her lip.

She not wrong, eh? Mama D'Leau said. She tilted her head at the mermaids, who deposited the children and swam off. Seaweed wrapped around their ankles and held them in place again. *And anyway, the fire burn two nights and one day. It mostly done already. Nothing you can do now. So hush.* She came to Corinne and placed a long finger beneath her chin. *Well?*

I did everything you asked, Corinne said.

Mama D'Leau's eyes settled on the three mermaids. *Not everything.*

We tried— Corinne began.

Tried? Mama D'Leau said. *Why don't I try something too, eh?*

Dru screamed. Her feet were suddenly rough and gray. The gray spread up to her ankles and then inched toward her knees. She was turning to stone.

Stop! Corinne yelled. *You promised to take us to the missing children!*

I bargain with you. Not them, Mama D'Leau said.

As the stone reached Dru's knees, Malik began to scream. His feet were turning to stone, too.

You won't get what you want, Bouki said. *We won't give you the stone.*

What make you think I can't just take it, Mama D'Leau said.

How? Bouki asked. *You don't know where it is.*

Mama D'Leau narrowed her eyes. *What you mean?*

I mean I hid it, he said. *And if you don't stop hurting them, you will never find it.*

The water churned and became an ominous dark gray at the same time as Mama D'Leau's eyes. *What if I kill one of them anyway? Real slow so you can't stand it.*

Malik and Dru continued to scream. Bouki's lower lip trembled but he kept silent. The jumbie's eye twitched and she turned away in one sweeping motion. The water calmed, and the stone flesh that had crept up Dru's and Malik's bodies faded away.

I will show you where I put it, Bouki said. *After they are safe on land.*

Bouki, you can't— Corinne began.

Now! Bouki shouted.

Mama D'Leau clapped her hands and Corinne, Dru, and Malik were ripped from the seaweed and tossed toward the island. They washed up on the gritty sand with ash raining down on them. The beach was empty. Corinne was exhausted, but she grabbed Malik and Dru and pulled them to their feet. Malik looked over at the sea, but Corinne turned him around.

"We need help to save Bouki," she said. "And there's no time to waste."

28

Two Cons

Bouki's heart beat hard, but he kept his face steady as Mama D'Leau coiled her tail beneath her body and sat heavily on top of it. *I could kill you, you know,* she said.

But you will never find your jewel, Bouki said.

I can taste your sweat in the water, Mama D'Leau said, laughing.

Bouki's heart did a triple beat. This was not going to be like his usual stare-down with people trying to cheat him. Mama D'Leau was formidable. But he reminded himself that all he had to do was wait her out. Even a jumbie had to lose her patience sometime.

Mama D'Leau's eyes narrowed, and she brought her fists down on the dead coral. Chunks of it broke away.

Why did you hide it? she asked.

I know a con when I see one, he said. *The others might not have seen it, but you can't swindle me so easily. I'm too old for that.*

Mama D'Leau swam close and brushed her long tail against his skin and over the top of his curly head. *Just old enough, I think.* She grinned.

Bouki stiffened. He remembered the white witch's warning. But he also knew that this was just another one of Mama D'Leau's tactics to scare him and rattle his plan. *You don't need me for a husband.*

Who said I need them? Mama D'Leau asked. *So where is it?*

You're in a big hurry, Bouki said.

You worried? I wouldn't hurt you.

At least not until I hand over the jewel, Bouki said.

You have brains, boy. I'll give you that.

Bouki tried not to look pleased. She might use it as another opportunity to pounce. He cleared his throat. *There's something I don't understand.*

What? About them? She turned toward the mermaids, who swam in a circle laughing and chattering.

No. You didn't have that stone for a long time. You don't need it.

Mama D'Leau shrugged. *Is mine. I miss it.*

The real thing I want to know is whether you and Mami Wata are the same.

Mama D'Leau whipped around and everything turned pitch-black. All Bouki could see was her wide, white smile.

29

The Ash Trees

Malik, Dru, and Corinne ran up the hill, coughing in the smoke-filled air, and burst into Corinne's house. It was empty, and Corinne could not hide her disappointment. Before they went back to the road, Corinne picked guavas from a small tree in the yard and tossed them to her friends. It was early for guava, and the thick green flesh was crisp, but sweet enough. The pink insides were heavy on Corinne's tongue. She sucked around the little seeds and spat them out as she ran.

Midway up the road people passed buckets of water to douse the flames. Corinne gasped at the sight of a lagahoo at the front of the line. The jumbie was twice the height of any person around it. Its teeth dripped saliva and its spiky fur heaved over its muscles. The chains around its neck clinked as it turned and saw Corinne.

She skidded to a stop and fell backward in the dusty road. A half-eaten guava fell from her hand and rolled to the lagahoo's huge paw. The fruit speared itself on a clump of the beast's coarse fur.

The lagahoo bared its teeth at the person behind it on the bucket line: Corinne's papa. Malik reached into his back pocket where his slingshot usually was and came up empty. Corinne scrambled to her feet and grabbed the guavas out of Dru's and Malik's hands. She ran screaming and pelting fruit at the lagahoo. It turned to her and growled.

"Corinne!" her papa cried. He ran and lifted her high off the ground into his arms. "You're safe!" His tears mixed with the ash on his face, streaking him black and brown. Behind Pierre, Mrs. Rootsingh reached for Dru and folded her daughter into her soft arms.

"Watch out!" Corinne looked for something else to attack the lagahoo with.

"No, Corinne. They are helping." Pierre put her down and stepped back so she could see.

The early morning light was still dim, but Corinne could make out several jumbies passing buckets of water. Douens were helping Hugo pull the buckets from the well, and two smaller lagahoo passed them along. The largest one was taking the bucket in its mouth and throwing water above the trees, where the people on the line could not reach.

The lagahoo passed the empty bucket to Mrs. Rootsingh.

"They really are helping," Dru said.

Malik pulled off to the back of the line and dove at the baker's neck. Hugo dropped to his knees, and then he looked toward the sea where Malik pointed and began to sob. Mrs. Rootsingh passed the next pail carefully to the lagahoo as she held Dru to her chest. She kissed Dru's head and swept her uneven hair behind her ears, leaving a trail of soot on her cheeks.

When the biggest lagahoo twisted its body to throw more water on the fire, it grimaced. There was singed fur and raw, exposed flesh on its front legs. It returned the empty container, baring its teeth again. Corinne went in closer, holding her papa's hand. She passed the next one to the jumbie herself, placing it carefully on the sharp teeth behind its black lips. The creature's large eyes shone. It blinked slowly and turned, throwing water over the trees.

"What is this?" A booming voice rang out behind them. It was Victor, one of the fishermen. In his hand was the same large metal hook he carried the day that Mama D'Leau had taken the children.

Pierre stepped between Victor and those working to put out the fire. "Go home, Victor."

Victor aimed his hook at the lagahoo at the front of the line. "It's their kind who caused all of this, Pierre," he said.

"They didn't set the fire," Pierre said.

"So now you have your child back, the rest don't matter?" He looked Corinne straight in the eye. "Did that jumbie show you where the children are?"

Everyone stopped and looked at Corinne. She bit her lip and shook her head. "She didn't—"

"You see? They took our children, and then they took our gifts, and what do we have to show for it?" He planted his feet and faced the first lagahoo. "They don't belong here. They are not like us. They are savage." Victor's lips were set in a long, hard line, and his forehead puckered as he stared the jumbie down. "I could do this myself. None of you can see sense."

"There is no sense in harming them," Pierre said. "It's not their fault. And now you've destroyed their homes."

"And you've put our homes in jeopardy," Mrs. Rootsingh added.

"You are all fools!" Victor shouted. "You can't fathom how cruel these jumbies are, because your child is one of them, Pierre. Your wife tricked you. But *they* can't trick everyone on the island." He took a running jump and brought the hook around and over his head. It curved toward the lagahoo. Pierre pulled Corinne out of the way as Victor's hook caught on one of the lagahoo's claws with a screeching sound like metal on metal. The lagahoo's paw and Victor's hook stuck in the dirt road just inches from Corinne's feet.

Without thinking, Corinne jumped on Victor's back and wrapped her hands over his face. Malik pried Victor's fingers away from the hook, as the lagahoo pulled its paw out. It licked at a fresh trickle of blood between its claws. Victor shook Corinne off him. He lowered his head and squared his shoulders. Pierre pushed Corinne to Mrs. Rootsingh and stepped in front of his friend.

"You would fight me for them?" Victor asked. "We have known each other since we were boys."

"You were wiser then," Pierre said.

Victor nodded and wiped his mouth against his shoulder. "When the island goes down, remember, you didn't do anything to stop it."

"I know you're angry, Victor," Pierre said. "But anger only makes more anger. Like fire only makes more fire. It doesn't help."

Victor glanced at Malik, who had picked up the gleaming hook and walked away.

The fire was a mere crackle now. No one could reach the remaining flames without walking through the smoldering forest, where branches fell, sending up red embers and hot ash. Everyone stopped and encircled Corinne, Malik, and Dru.

"Didn't she tell you anything about the missing children?" Mrs. Rootsingh asked.

"No, Mama," Dru said. "She sent us on an errand to get a stone. But . . ." She looked at Corinne.

"Bouki hid the stone because he didn't trust her," Corinne said. "So she took him."

"Why would he do that?" Hugo asked.

"He saved us, Uncle," Corinne said. "She wasn't going to hold up her end of the bargain."

"And now a fourth child is gone," Hugo said. He pulled Malik to his side.

"And we have no way to get any of them back," Mrs. Rootsingh said.

An argument rose into the air like smoke, about what could be done and what they should have done in the first place.

Dru pulled Corinne and Malik away. "They'll never figure it out with all that yelling." She threw a look at her mother. "We have to get Mama D'Leau to keep her end of the bargain."

"We could ask the mermaids," Corinne suggested.

Malik shook his head.

"There's only one jumbie Mama D'Leau will listen to, and he's in there," Dru said. They looked at the smoky forest.

"How do we get him to come out?" Corinne asked.

"I'm not sure Papa Bois ever leaves the forest," Dru said. She played with the ends of her hair and pulled a strand toward her lips.

"Then we will have to go in," Corinne said.

"It's too dangerous," Dru said.

"That hasn't stopped us before."

As the three of them made a plan, the adults' argument petered out.

Pierre came to Corinne. "There's nothing more we can do for now," he said. "We can only hope that the fire doesn't catch again, or that the rain comes."

Small flickers still burned, but they would have to wait for parts of the forest to cool before continuing on. Gaping holes had been burned into the wall of orange trees that Corinne and the white witch had planted to separate jumbies and people. Animals were scurrying out through the gaps, but behind the trees, scores of others cried out, scratching from the other side. The tree wall was strong and held most of them inside the steaming forest. Corinne felt sick to her stomach. She had made the wall. She had trapped the animals inside. She had done this.

Mrs. Rootsingh held out her hands for Dru. Malik joined Hugo on the road to the bakery. People returned to their villages, and the jumbies skirted the forest, looking for a safe place to enter. When they did, they stamped out flickers of orange flame with their feet and hooves. Both people and jumbies looked to the sky. The sun had just risen, and heavy clouds dimmed the light, but they gave no rain.

Corinne put her sooty hand into her father's and rubbed his rough skin. They trudged to the house on the hill, where Pierre made Corinne clean herself up. He gave her something warm to eat and ushered her to bed. The sun had just risen over the sea. But when Corinne saw him return to the front room to watch the fire, she joined him. She laid her head in her papa's lap and looked at the forest. She felt his hands and the pull of a comb as Pierre untangled knots and plaited her hair. The rhythm of each stroke of the comb and Pierre's fingers against her locks after each pass soothed her. Before long, she fell asleep.

• • •

Later in the morning, the bittersweet scent of burned wood filled the air. White ash had blown in through the open door and windows. Corinne kicked a blanket off her legs, and ash drifted to the floor. It left streaks everywhere—on the furniture, the shelves, even the broken wax figure of Corinne's mama. She found her papa in the garden, walking among the plants and shaking the ash off leaves and branches. Everything was covered in a delicate layer of white, as if someone had sprinkled salt over it all, even Corinne's oranges.

"They will choke," Pierre said.

Corinne followed him, shaking ash off some plants, blowing or wiping it from others. When they were finished, Corinne prepared eggs and tea while Pierre sliced bread. They ate quickly, and without a word, got dressed and went to the mahogany forest. When they bent the corner from their house and started on the straight part of the road to the dry well, Corinne gasped. Pierre squeezed her shoulder and steered her forward.

The forest was black. Wisps of smoke curled from its depths, and the shrubs that had edged the trees and grown up anywhere they could find space had become tangles of blackened twigs. The wall of orange trees was still standing, but the burned-out holes ringed with black were starker in daylight.

Pierre and Corinne reached the tamarind tree where Corinne had once faced off against a sharp-toothed lagahoo. She wondered if it was the same big one that had helped them the night before. The tree's branches were broken, and many of the tamarind pods lay on the ground, roasted. Corinne picked one up and it broke apart in her hand. It smelled smoky and sweet.

"What if Laurent and the others were in the forest, Papa?" she asked.

Pierre took a breath. "Setting the fire was a bad thing to do. Parents were afraid for their children and hurt because nothing they tried had worked. Fear and sorrow can make anyone do foolish things." His voice was strained. "Wherever the children are, this didn't help." He wiped a hand across Corinne's furrowed brow. "But if

Mama D'Leau said she would take you to them, it means they could not have been on land. We will find them, Corinne. Somehow."

Hugo was sitting on a bench in front of the bakery. His kind face looked drawn and sallow. He and Pierre went inside, and Malik replaced him on the bench. Corinne sat with him. They focused their attention on the road that led to Dru's village and waited.

"Malik," Corinne said. "I'm sorry about yelling at you."

Malik smiled a very small smile then refocused on the road. A few minutes later Dru appeared around the corner. They met her and raced to where the line of orange trees met the thickest part of the forest.

Corinne found a hole large enough for all of them to go through.

30

Papa Bois

Smoke irritated their noses, and a low sizzle was still in the air. The ground was hot and sandals provided little protection. The rubber soles stuck to the burned forest floor. Fewer leaves and branches meant more light, but the smoldering carcasses of trees made the mahogany forest a graveyard of broken black bones reaching to the sky. The sky that hung over them was still cloudy and withheld even a hint of blue.

Corinne was used to the feeling of many eyes on her, especially when she stepped into the woods, but today the forest felt empty. Somehow, that was worse. She heard the sharp crack of a twig to her left and spun in that direction.

Corinne and her friends stood still, barely breathing, waiting for another sound.

"Papa Bois?" Corinne called out softly.

"No, not Papa."

Corinne's stomach tightened.

Something small stirred behind the fallen trunk of a tree that had been split down the middle. The little thing came around, kicking up ash and a few tiny embers until it faced Corinne, Dru, and Malik.

"Allan!" Dru rushed to her friend. Allan was nearly naked except for the round hat that the douens wore and the last shreds of the pants he was wearing the night the jumbies had taken him. They hung off his hips beneath a round belly. "You're alive!" Dru cried, hugging him and looking back at the others. Corinne frowned and Dru pulled away to look at Allan's backward-facing feet.

Corinne pulled Dru away. When Severine had sent jumbies to attack the people of the island, Allan had been taken. But Corinne wasn't sure how, exactly, so she didn't want Dru to get too close.

Several more douens came out from behind burned-out trees and ash-covered stumps. They surrounded the children.

"It's not safe here," Allan said.

"Are you going to eat us?" Dru asked.

"I won't hurt you," Allan said.

Malik pointed at the closing circle of douens.

"What about them?" Corinne asked.

Allan didn't say.

"But last night everyone was working together," Corinne said.

Allan shrugged. "Last night was different."

"We have a message for Papa Bois," Dru said. "Can you help us?"

The advancing douens paused, and Allan tilted his head up so that they could see his face. A chill went through Corinne. Allan looked so much like his mother, Mrs. Ramdeen.

"There are children missing," Corinne said. "Like you. Papa Bois can help us get them back home."

Allan's eyes narrowed. "I can't go home," he said. "No one has helped me. Not even Papa Bois."

"Your mama has been searching for you every day," Dru said.

"She will never find me. I don't want her to see me now. She will hate me, just like the people who did this." He gestured around to the blackened trees. "I'm learning to sense when people come near. That's how I found you." He looked at Dru. "You didn't come looking for me. You were my friend. Do you hate me, too?"

"Nobody hates you, Allan," Corinne said. "The people who set the fire were angry and scared because too many children have gone missing, including you. We have to find all of them, and only Papa Bois can help us with that."

"We can get everyone home with your help," Dru said.

"I miss my soft bed. And my mama's pelau," he whispered.

"So you will help us?" Corinne asked.

Allan ran awkwardly to Corinne with his backward feet and grabbed her hand. He pulled her over the smoking ground. Corinne tried to twist her way out of his grip, but it was like a vise. Malik and Dru followed with the douens close on their heels. Allan stopped in front of a large, squat boulder surrounded by a few trees that seemed to have been spared from the fire. Several branches were full of unfurling leaves of bright, fresh green. "Here," he said.

"What is here?" Dru asked.

Allan pointed at the rock.

Corinne felt something like a heartbeat coming up through the soles of her sandals. It was as if the entire forest had come alive. The pulse felt stronger as she moved closer to the boulder. She squinted at it and turned her head to the side. The boulder itself moved as if it was breathing. Corinne's pulse quickened, but she reached a finger out to touch it, and the surface felt soft but tough, like muscle. She jumped back. The boulder rearranged itself. Cracks and crevices twisted in other directions. Some opened up, exposing new muscle beneath, and the surface of the rock shifted. When it stopped moving, the boulder had unfolded into a little old man not much taller than Corinne, with a long gray beard, the legs of a goat, and a pair of tiny horns peeking through his messy gray cornrowed hair.

Dru grabbed Corinne's arm, and Corinne stared agape at Papa Bois's hoofed feet until Malik tipped her chin up to meet his eyes.

"What are you staring at?" the old man asked in a voice like the long, slow creaking of timber.

Dru took a deep breath. "Sorry, sir," she said, her voice trembling. "Good morning, sir." Then she added, "We need your help."

"I know that already," Papa Bois said, taking his time for each word. He settled against a walking stick, which a moment before had looked like a branch that had fallen against the rock. "So, which of you was it that started the fire?"

"None of us," Corinne said. "Sir," she added. "We weren't here when the fire was set. We don't know—"

Papa Bois held up his walking stick. He looked at Dru. "She came with her matches and set fire to the wood. I can still smell the sulfur on her fingers. She had long hair then. But I took care of that." Papa Bois moved slowly in the little clearing as he spoke. He bent over the few surviving plants and picked up a half-burned leaf. In his fingers, it sprang back to life. He looked at Dru again. "Not so?"

She pulled at the shaggy edges of her shiny black hair and looked down at the ground. "Yes, sir," she said. "But that was a little while ago. And I didn't mean for the fire to get out of hand. And I'm sorry, sir."

"But here we are again." Papa Bois gestured around them.

"This time it wasn't her," Corinne said.

"A fire is a fire," Papa Bois said. "Burn one tree, burn one hundred, it's all the same unless you are burning it for warmth or to cook your food. It's wasteful."

"She was trying to help me," Corinne said.

"And while she did that, she was hurting others." Papa Bois's stare rooted Corinne to the ground. She felt as trapped as she had been in the grip of Mama D'Leau's seaweed. "Someone will have to pay," he said.

Corinne stepped forward. "If anyone should pay, it's me."

Papa Bois chuckled slowly. A few tears squeezed out of the wrinkled corners of his kind brown eyes. Where they fell to the ground, tiny white flowers sprang up and opened their buds. "Tell me, did Mama D'Leau send you for her treasure?"

Corinne felt her muscles go slack. "How do you know about that?"

"I can smell the sea on you," he said. "It goes right through you. Like you've been soaking in it." He put his hand on the bark of a tree, and it changed from ashen gray to deep brown. "The help you need has something to do with Mama D'Leau, I bet."

"She has Malik's brother, sir," Dru said.

"And Mama D'Leau promised to show us where some missing children are," Corinne said. "But she didn't keep her promise."

"She listens to you, doesn't she?" Dru asked.

Papa Bois tilted his head and looked at Malik. "It's nice to be quiet, isn't it? You see so much more than the others." He winked and walked on. Beneath his hooves, grass shot up and bushes grew with every brush of his fingers. Even the soil became springy beneath him. Gradually, the black-and-white world of the forest was coming alive again.

Malik pointed to the light waning in the sky.

"How did it get so late?" Dru asked.

"Things take time to heal," Papa Bois said. "Nothing happens quickly."

"We have to get back," Corinne said. "Mama D'Leau still has Bouki, and she—"

"She won't hurt him, if he's smart and he keeps his mouth shut."

Corinne swallowed hard, Dru's shoulders drooped, and Malik's lips twisted.

"I see," Papa Bois said. "Better get on with it then." The sky was already turning orange.

"How is this happening?" Corinne asked. "We will never get there by sunset. It's the only time we can call her."

"Don't worry, sapling," Papa Bois said. "It's not as far as you think." He tilted his head and closed his eyes as if he was trying to hear something from far away. "She is ready now, little ones. Hold on."

Corinne felt the earth move around her. The ground opened up and swallowed them, burying them in sediment and roots. Soil pressed so hard against her she couldn't breathe. Then they shifted sideways, going through rocks, past earthworms and ants, centipedes and scorpions, until the earth fell away again and they were standing in the same positions as before, only they were no longer in the forest. They were at the edge of the sea, and several people on the beach looked shocked by their sudden arrival.

Corinne, Malik, and Dru panted.

Papa Bois looked at a man who had his hands around the neck of a small rabbit. "Are you planning to eat that, son?"

The man's grip slackened, and the rabbit stopped screaming and dropped to the ground. People ran off toward the village, while the rabbit bounded toward the cliff.

Corinne called up to her house. "Papa!"

Pierre and Hugo came running out the back. They disappeared inside the house and reappeared on the path to the beach. Their faces were frantic with worry. When they got close enough, they pulled Corinne, Dru, and Malik into their arms and away from Papa Bois.

"It's okay, Papa," Corinne said. "He is here to help us."

"Why did you leave?" Hugo scolded Malik. He shook Malik gently at the shoulders, then pulled him into a hug. "You could have been hurt!" he said. He kept holding Malik away from his body and pulling him close over and over again as if he wasn't sure that he was really there, safe and sound. Then he turned to Dru. "Your mother has been very upset."

Dru lowered her eyes.

"How is he going to help?" Pierre asked.

Papa Bois picked up his walking stick and pointed across the water. The sun had just touched the sea, and a large wave rose up and hurtled toward them.

31

Water and Sand

The surge dissipated just before reaching shore, and in the middle of it, Mama D'Leau rose up to her waist. Her long braids hung around her body with shells and seaweed knotted in the strands like the tangle of Pierre's nets when he hauled them from the sea.

"So you come then," Mama D'Leau said. Her voice rolled like a wave over the onlookers.

"I hear you just fine," said Papa Bois.

"With them old ears?" Mama D'Leau asked with a laugh.

"They are the same age as yours, about," he replied.

"But you brought them with you." Mama D'Leau sneered at the children.

"These are friends of mine," Papa Bois said. "They have asked for my help. Seems you have someone of theirs."

Mama D'Leau nodded. "I have something else, too. Meet me at the edge."

Papa Bois moved forward. Mama D'Leau skimmed along the top of a wave as it rumbled to the beach. As they got closer to each other, the jumbies' bodies began to change. Papa Bois's legs and back straightened out, making him appear taller, and his hooves became bare feet with anklets of twisted vines.

Mama D'Leau's tail separated into legs and the water clung around her like a sparkling silver dress.

Papa Bois's face changed too. The white beard disappeared, and his hair darkened. Each cornrow was twisted with twigs and leaves. His eyes never changed. They were still twinkling and dark against his bark-brown skin as he arrived at the edge of the water with the sea slipping past his toes.

With no tail to lengthen her body, Mama D'Leau was only a little taller than Papa Bois. Her copper skin gleamed, while her eyes flashed the same golden color as the sea under the setting sun. She stood in the barest edge of a wave, just in front of Papa Bois. They looked like any other man or woman, only more beautiful than any two people Corinne had ever seen before.

The sun sank beneath the waves and both of them were cast in an orange glow. Mama D'Leau reached up into the pile of hair wrapped at the top of her head, and pulled out the stone Bouki had hidden. "It's the ocean," she explained. "See? This is what it is like under the water."

He nodded and laughed. "I see. It's both of us. Land and sea."

"Together," she said.

He took the stone from her and looked at it carefully. "Thank you."

Mama D'Leau bowed gracefully.

Malik made a face like he was going to throw up.

"Oh no, do you think they're going to kiss? It looks like they're going to kiss. Disgusting." Everyone spun toward the sound of Bouki's voice.

He pulled himself out of the water, looking like a half-drowned cat.

Hugo splashed into the sea and gathered Bouki up, laughing and hugging him. "You should not have done what you did!" Hugo said angrily. "You could have died!"

"Sorry," Bouki said. "Malik and I will leave. We won't bother you again."

"Leave to go where?" Hugo asked.

"You're mad at us, so we will go," Bouki said. "Back to the caves."

Hugo's huge body softened. "You are going nowhere, son. We will always be together. You will just have to stand here and let me yell at you." He hugged Bouki again.

"I prefer the yelling," Bouki whined. "*She* already squeezed me half to death."

Hugo let go of Bouki and hugged Malik instead.

By the time Corinne looked at the jumbies again, they were moving away from each other and transforming back into their usual selves. Mama D'Leau's tail unfurled beneath her, and she grew tall again. Papa Bois leaned on his cane and his back bent with age as his beard flowed down his bare chest.

Mama D'Leau turned to Corinne. "You did what I asked, so I will hold up my end of the bargain." She reached out and Corinne walked to her.

"I'm coming with you," Pierre said.

The white witch gripped Pierre's shoulder with her good hand. Corinne had not seen her arrive on the beach. She shook her head at both of them.

"My deal is with her alone," Mama D'Leau said. "But don't worry, eh? *I* won't harm her."

Fear gripped Corinne as Mama D'Leau pulled her under the water and out to sea.

You are taking me to them, Corinne said.

I'm taking you to her, Mama D'Leau said.

Her.

Don't act stupid, Corinne. You know exactly who I mean.

So she survived, Corinne said.

Mama D'Leau snorted. *Of course she did. Did you think you could stop a jumbie?*

32

Lagoon des Enfants

Mama D'Leau pulled Corinne over coral reefs and past slow-moving manatees and leatherback turtles. They crossed the foul-smelling section of water where the witch's swamp emptied into the sea. One unfortunate little fish got just close enough and Mama D'Leau reached out and caught it mid-dive. She tore into it with her teeth until there was nothing left, not even a bone or one shimmering scale. She felt Corinne's disgust. *Hungry?* she asked.

Corinne shook her head no. *The mermaids were different when we crossed the ocean,* she said.

So?

It all started after we found a sunken ship.

Mmm hmm.

They showed me what happened to them on that ship.

Mama D'Leau ground her teeth. *They couldn't have.*

They did. I saw it. I felt them drown. You erased their memories so they wouldn't know who they were. But when they got home, they started to remember their families and the lives they had. They were so sad that Ellie—

Imagine if they remembered that pain all the time, Mama D'Leau said. *How you think they would survive that, eh? How many can survive being ripped from their family and friends, forever torn apart?* She tugged Corinne along roughly. *Memories are painful.*

You pruned them, Corinne said.

What you mean, prune?

I mean, you cut off the part of their memory that was hurting them. You didn't think it was something they needed. You were trying to help.

Ridiculous. Why I would do that?

Because you were lonely.

Mama D'Leau blew water from her nose. She had missed the entrance to the lagoon. *Stop talking. You too distracting.*

You treat them like your children. That's because you chose them. Like Bouki and Malik are Uncle Hugo's children now, but they weren't always. You wanted the mermaids for your family.

Mama D'Leau had never missed the inlet before. Everything was so much quieter without the girl chattering in her ears. People were so much better as stones. *Sometimes family is a choice you make,* she said. *And other times they are a burden you bear. It's a gamble. Sometimes it works out.*

And sometimes it doesn't.

Mama D'Leau heard Severine's song rippling out, and made a sharp turn into a narrow stream, following it. The water stilled and was less salty there. It reflected the rising moon and filtered light to the waving plants below. Mama D'Leau watched two Corinnes staring at each other in the glassy surface.

Severine continued to sing.

Hush sweetheart, oh my darling,
Fall asleep now, time to rest.
Waves push and pull the cradle
Gently in your water nest.

The water songs were powerful, but the girl seemed stronger. Mama D'Leau felt Corinne willing herself not to listen.

Where are we? Corinne asked.

The people on the island call it lagoon des enfants, Mama D'Leau said. *Your friends are not the first little ones trapped beneath the water here, but they may be the first to survive. You see, it doesn't look dangerous from the top. Nor deep neither. And the small silver fish real charming. Little ones love to try and catch them, but the ground sticky and slippery, and the current pulls strong.*

Mama D'Leau stopped in the middle of the lagoon and pointed toward a shadowy corner. *They all waiting there,* she said. *Your friends, and . . . your* tante.

How did you know she is my aunt?

I have been here a long time, Corinne. I can smell the family in your blood, and I can see them in your body and the way you move. You have your father's kind eyes, and your mother's courage, and your tante's stubborn streak.

I don't, Corinne said.

Why didn't Ellie come back, Corinne? Mama D'Leau asked.

She—

No, not she. You, Mama D'Leau said. *You could have stopped her.*

I tried to save her, Corinne said.

Dead is dead. What would you do for the ones you love? No less than me, I expect. Mama D'Leau let go of Corinne. She waited to feel the current pull Corinne down with its invisible fingers. The vibration of Corinne's panic mingled with Severine's song and tickled Mama D'Leau's skin.

Gently gently, darling doux doux,
Hard upon the rocks we fall.
Water takes away the broken
Bones and hearts and memories all.

Mama D'Leau felt Corinne's lungs empty of air, and her muscles tire and grow as slack as the waving plants beneath her. The water washed Corinne toward a cave in the shadows.

Mama D'Leau laughed.

33

Favorite Food

The little douen broke free of the pack and ran along the uneven ground of the forest. Charred bits of wood cracked and turned to dust beneath his feet as he went. His tough muscles helped him break through burned-out trunks of trees and scarred shrubs as easily as if he was running through his mama's sheets hanging from a line. He reached the outskirts of his old village and waited.

"Allan!" Mrs. Ramdeen called out. Her voice cracked like twigs under a heel. "Allan!"

He was beginning to feel her better than he could see her. He still had his eyes, not like the other douens, but he felt her heart thrumming first, faster and faster, as she came into the forest, and he could smell her warm, salty skin and the blood that ran underneath. He smelled the cooking on her, too. Pelau. She held a bowl of it in one hand and as she walked, trembling with fright, grains of rice, bits of sweet round peas, and pieces of seasoned meat fell to the ground, leaving a trail that Allan ate after her. Pelau was his favorite.

This time he did not let her go off alone. This time he allowed himself to get closer. If she turned around, she might just make him out in the shadows. But she could not sense him like he could sense her. And after a while, she returned to the village.

Allan ate the last of the pelau. He felt someone else deeper in the forest and followed their frantic thrumming heart. He arrived at the open lagoon just in time to see Corinne disappear under the water, being pulled down as if by a current. There were others down there, too. Little ones dreaming of their mothers' cooking. Maybe it was not too late for them.

34

Tante Severine

The moonlight disappeared and Corinne was plunged into darkness once again. She looked around, hoping to spot something she could grab on to, anything that might help her rise to the surface, to air, before it was too late. Her eyes began to pick up subtle shades in the water. Then the lagoon lit up the way the sea did when Corinne had touched Sisi's hand, only she was on her own now. She blinked a few times to make sure she wasn't imagining it, and reached out and caught a reed with blue and purple along its edges and yellow running through its veins. She could see like a jumbie, but she still couldn't breathe underwater. And there was still the pull of the song that made her want to relax, to let go.

Corinne's fingers loosened and the current took her into the cave where rocks glittered on the sandy floor, and the sides shone. They reminded her of her mama's stone and how it had glowed when she needed it most. She felt the stone pulling against her, but even her mama's necklace could not pry her away from the water's hold. It was no use going against the tide, her papa had said.

Corinne's lungs burned. She wished she could see her papa's face one more time, but her mama was here, and she could kiss her. She brought the stone to her lips. The current shifted and the stone slipped into her mouth. Corinne spat it out, realizing that for that one moment, she could breathe. But when the stone was gone, so was her breath. She put the stone in her mouth again, and her lungs filled with air.

The current tapered off, leaving Corinne adrift in the middle of the dark cave. The song came from one of several small openings that led farther back. Corinne followed it to a large chamber where glowing rocks illuminated the faces of three sleeping children—and Severine.

She was not as Corinne remembered. The beautiful woman who had awed everyone at the market was gone. But so, too, was the creature made of wood with insects crawling into and through her flesh that Corinne had fought on the cliff. What was left was something in between—a woman with dark, shining eyes and flesh as hard and smooth as driftwood. The tattered remains of her green dress floated around her like tentacles. Her hair had come undone and waved like a black crown around her face. Something about her was still beautiful, but also frightening.

You've come, Severine said. She smiled happily as if the last time she had seen Corinne had been pleasant. She took Corinne's hand and led her to the sleeping children. Up close, Corinne saw that their throats were glowing orange.

Sister's child, Severine said, *we have another chance to bring everyone to our side. Look how easy it was to get these.*

Corinne went to Laurent. He was wearing the same white shirt and blue shorts as on the day of the earthquake. Now Corinne could see that it was not his throat that was glowing, but something inside it shining through.

Now that you are here, it will be easier, Severine said. *Parents have been keeping the children away from the water. But you can bring them to the edge. They know you. They trust you.*

Laurent's head lolled forward, and Severine smoothed it back.

You're hurting them, Corinne said.

No, no, Severine said. *See? They are fine. They are happy. And now you are here, and I am happy too.*

Corinne shook her head. *You hate me,* she said. *You tried to turn my father into a jumbie.*

Like you, Severine said. *He would have been just like you. No. He couldn't think. He wasn't my papa.*

Severine frowned as if she was trying to understand. *But it would not have been that way for long,* she said. *As soon as you joined us—*

You would have killed everyone on the island! Corinne said.

Something of the anger that Corinne remembered flitted across Severine's face, making her frown. Then she relaxed again. *We have a better plan now,* she said, waving her hand toward the children. *Now everyone will come to us.*

We? Corinne sputtered. The leather-wrapped rock dislodged from her mouth, and she had to put it in again. *This is not my plan.*

Of course it is! Severine said. *You showed me how families would never be split up. You came to get your mama's necklace, and you fought for your papa. Their mothers and fathers will do the same. They will come looking for them. And when they find them—*

No!

Wickedness pooled into Severine's eyes. *Yes. And all because of you,* she said.

I will stop you, Corinne said.

Like you did last time? Severine floated closer to Corinne. *Look how much better it is. Here you are, underwater, in a dark cave, seeing just as well as I see, breathing, surviving all because of your mama's stone. It's missing a piece, isn't it?* Severine reached into her own throat and pulled out a shard that glowed the same orange as Corinne's, the same color as the things inside the children's throats. The jumbie smiled wickedly. *The whole piece was too strong for me. But this little shard has been helpful. Thank you, sister's child. You have given me everything. Even some new children to take. I can feel them by the water.*

Corinne thought of Dru, Malik, and Bouki waiting on the beach. Her chest tightened. Not only had she failed to get rid of Severine, but she had given Severine a way to capture and hold on to her friends. She had shown Severine that the children's families would not abandon them. And now she had lined up the people she cared about most at the edge of the water to be captured. Nothing she had done helped. And in the process, she had begun to feel more like jumbie than girl.

Marlene stirred, and Severine leaned over and fixed the ribbon in her hair as she sang,

Come and join us in the water,
Sing a chorus to the waves.
Skip the current, rope the seaweed,
Play among the fishes' graves.

The water's song makes them forget, Severine said. *And when they forget, they don't struggle so much. I learned it from the mermaids when I was trapped under the rocks. I listened to*

them sing away the memories of the fishermen who saw them. They were beautiful songs. I was beginning to forget, too. And I stopped trying to escape. And then the earthquake came and every memory shook out with it. I remembered you, Corinne. I remembered how in the end, you had tried to help me. Because that is family. Family forgives. And I forgive you, niece.

Corinne felt the weight of all her failures press her body down like water at the bottom of the sea. Worry closed in on her like shadows. What was there left to do?

She reached for Severine's outstretched hand. *I forgive you too, Tante Severine.*

35

A Breath of Water

Severine smiled. Corinne saw hope creep into her aunt's eyes, and she felt a stab of guilt.

Watch them, Severine said. *I will get your friends.*

As soon as Severine was gone, Corinne tried to wake Laurent. He opened his eyes wide and gasped for air. Corinne tried to stop him, to talk to him, but he only thrashed around. She hummed, trying to recall the words of Severine's song, but in her panic she couldn't remember it exactly.

Come in the water,
Sing . . . sing to the waves.
Follow the current,
We'll play in the . . . graves?

Laurent opened his mouth to scream and swallowed water. Corinne tried to hold him steady and closed her eyes, humming again. This time she tried her own song.

Hush, friend, I came to save you.
Please be still and close your eyes.
One more trick, we'll swim away
From Severine's nasty lies.

As soon as Laurent became still, Corinne pulled him out of the cave. But the current made it almost impossible to tow him. She settled him on the rocks and buried her face in her hands.

The current changed slightly, the way it had when it brought her into the cave. It pulsed, like breathing. She pulled Laurent back onto her shoulder and waited for the next breath. Then she kicked out of the cave and to the surface.

Corinne dragged Laurent to the bank and tried to wake him up. His eyes flew open and he gasped again for air. At the same time, Corinne felt as if she was going to choke. She pulled out her mother's stone, snapping the cord as she did, but she was able to breathe again. She dropped the necklace and turned Laurent on his stomach. She thumped his back to dislodge the stone shard from his throat, but Laurent was struggling. He was going to drown in air, like a fish.

36

Familiar Ground

Allan returned to his village, walking on the smooth, uneven pitch where he used to shoot marbles with his friends. He passed familiar houses and approached one with no paint on the outside. He moved past the sleeping chickens and goats and scratched at the bottom of the Dutch door. He heard the tiptoe of a small pair of feet on the bare floor. A board creaked, and the feet moved more slowly.

Allan sank into the shadows and waited.

Dru opened the top of the door. She held a rolling pin in both hands. Moonlight fell across her face, highlighting her determined eyes and casting shadows beneath the jagged crops of black hair that fell against her cheeks.

Allan stepped into the light. "I know where the children are."

Dru lowered the rolling pin and opened the door wide. "Show me."

37

A Call for Help

Pierre stood next to his yellow boat and refused to leave the beach until Corinne returned.

"She's strong, Pierre," the white witch said. "Don't worry."

Still, Pierre would not budge. Hugo and the boys stayed with him long after everyone else had left. Bouki itched to do something, but he wasn't sure what would have helped. Besides, he didn't want to upset Hugo any more. The food and clean clothes and soft beds were nice for Malik. He didn't want to ruin it.

"So, what now?" the witch asked no one in particular.

Bouki turned and found Malik walking into the water. "What are you doing, brother?" he asked.

Malik touched his lips to the top of a wave and whispered, "Help."

38

Friend or Foe?

Dru shivered against the night as Allan tugged her along. Behind them the sound of voices was low at first, and then louder. Lamplight flickered through the charred trees like darting fireflies.

Torches blossomed in the dark, illuminating the angry faces of people picking their way through the forest, along with their pitchforks, fishing hooks, iron pots, and cricket bats.

"They are looking for us," Dru said.

Allan shook his head. "They are looking for *you*."

Allan stopped suddenly. Behind them, the douens had formed a half-circle, forcing the search party to stop.

< 213 >

"We have to help them," Dru said. "Or it will be just like the night we lost you."

A tiny whimper escaped from Allan's throat. Dru scanned the crowd, spotting her parents and then Mrs. Ramdeen.

"She will be happy to see you, Allan."

Allan chewed his lips. Finally, he stepped out, pulling Dru with him between the douens and the people from the village. On his backward feet, his toes dug hard into the ash-covered dirt.

"Dru," Mrs. Rootsingh said. "Careful!"

Allan faced the douens. "They want their children back."

One of the larger jumbies stepped forward. "Oh?" it asked. Its brothers took another step toward the crowd.

Mrs. Ramdeen moved to the front and held her arms open. "Allan?" she said.

"Dru, come," Mrs. Rootsingh said slowly.

The tall douen held out its hands to Dru and Allan.

"Please, no, doux doux," Mrs. Ramdeen cried.

The burned leaves under Allan's bare, backward feet crunched loudly in the silent forest. Dru held her breath. Allan lowered his head so only the top of his peaked hat could be seen above his shoulders, and he reached for the douen's hand. Mrs. Ramdeen dropped to her knees and wailed. The douens' mouths widened in satisfied smiles. They chanted, "Oh oh oh!" joyfully.

The sound made Dru feel light-headed. She rounded her lips to sing, too, but Allan pushed her toward her parents, snapping her out of her trance. "Oh oh oh oh oh oh oh!" the douens cried out.

"Go!" Allan yelled at Dru.

"The children are this way!" Dru said. She led her neighbors to the line of trees before the lagoon, but she didn't follow them through. Mrs. Ramdeen and Allan were still facing the douens.

"Keep going!" Mrs. Ramdeen shouted. "The children will want their mothers."

Dru thought of Laurent's mother waiting by the sea. She pulled her parents in that direction as Mrs. Ramdeen turned to face the douens with her son.

39

How to Breathe

I f Laurent did not get air soon, he would die on the bank of the lagoon. As he gasped for breath, the shard in his throat glowed brighter and brighter. Corinne tried to pull him back into the water. He kicked and clawed at her, his eyes huge and fearful.

"I'm trying to help, Laurent!" Corinne said. But he kept pushing her away.

"Stop!" Miss Evelyn ran out of the forest toward them. "What are you doing?"

Laurent stopped kicking to look back at the people emerging from the trees. Corinne made one final pull and took him down into the water. There wasn't time to explain. Miss Evelyn and a man from Dru's village dove in after them. Corinne tried to pull the shard out of Laurent's throat with her fingers. He bit down hard. She hit him in the chest with her other hand, and he coughed the shard out. Almost immediately, he started gasping again, but a pair of hands pulled him out of the water. Corinne watched him rise as the current pulled her back in.

She collected Gabrielle and Marlene. She had left her mama's stone on the shore, so she had to work fast. At the opening of the cave, she thumped the girls on the back and they coughed up the stone pieces. Then Corinne pushed them up into the hands of the adults, too.

She surfaced a few seconds later and took a deep breath.

Laurent was already on land. Marlene and Gabrielle were being carefully towed to shore. She had done it.

"There she is!" Miss Evelyn screamed. "Grab her! She tried to drown Laurent!"

The man turned back. His face was contorted with effort. Corinne took a large gulp of air and dove under. Her head buzzed, both with worry and from the effort of holding her breath. She searched desperately for one of the shards that could help her breathe. In spite of everything Corinne had done, Severine had returned, and she would be angry when she saw the children gone. Then there was Mama D'Leau. Corinne had made an enemy of her, too. Even the orange trees she had planted had trapped animals in the fire. Everything she had tried to do had harmed someone. None of her plans had worked. *Memories are painful,* Mama D'Leau had said. It was true. Corinne felt each remembered failure as if it was marked in her skin.

Maybe there was some kindness in what Mama D'Leau had done when she helped the mermaids to forget. A pair of hands grabbed Corinne and pulled her away from the cave and out of the water. Her first breath calmed her burning lungs, and with her second, she opened her eyes to the angry faces that awaited her on shore.

40

A Promise to Keep

Bouki tried to pull Malik out of the waves. "Hugo will be upset," he said.

Malik put a finger to his lips and looked behind his brother to the beach.

Victor moved right up to Pierre's face. "I told you that you should not have taken their side. Now you've helped them, and Corinne is gone again. We still don't know where the other children are."

"Step back, Victor," said the witch.

Victor pushed her away. "All of these jumbies need to go," he said. "This is our island. We have to get rid of them."

Pierre lifted his head. His eyes were like daggers. "Get rid of who? My child? The white witch?"

Victor squared his shoulders.

Malik pinched Bouki's arm and pointed at a long green tail fin in the water.

"Don't," Bouki said.

But Malik waded out, and Bouki followed, sighing.

"Didn't we do enough for you the last time?" Noyi asked. She sucked her teeth, *chups*.

"Corinne needs your help," Bouki said to Sisi. "Didn't you promise her grand-père to keep her out of trouble?"

"Mama D'Leau will not harm her," Sisi said.

"But she might leave her somewhere and she will get hurt," Bouki whispered. "And then you would not have kept your promise."

Sisi looked around as if someone under the water might hear them.

"If you're worried about Mama D'Leau, don't," Bouki said. "Parents always forgive, even when their children make them angry."

"She is not really our mother," Addie said.

"She chose you." Bouki glanced at Hugo. "It's the same thing. So, will you help us?"

41

Which Jumbie?

D ru arrived at Corinne's hill just as Pierre and Victor were about to face off. Her parents were just behind her. "We found them," she called. Her voice rang out over the beach and echoed off the cliff.

Laurent's mother, Mrs. Duval, darted from her house, calling, "Where is he? Where is he?"

The crowd hurried up the hill.

"They're at the lagoon," Dru said. "It's far. But if we run . . ."

"Why do we have to run?" Bouki asked.

"The lagoon is dangerous," Hugo said. "We have lost many children there." Then he looked around at the faces on the hill. "Where is Malik?"

"With the mermaids," Bouki said. Before Hugo could protest or get angry again, Bouki put his hand on Hugo's large arm. "He will be fine. They like *him*."

Hugo looked confused.

"They're taking him to Corinne, and they move fast, so he will probably be there long before us."

"If Corinne found them, why didn't she come to tell us?" Mrs. Duval asked.

"She's probably in trouble again," said the white witch.

"How, when she is one of *them*," Victor spat.

"One who risked herself again and again to help her friends?" the witch asked. "Yes, she is one of *them*."

They moved quickly up the road past the dry well, but when they reached the full one, Bouki paused. "Do you hear that?"

"What? I don't hear anything," the witch said.

"*You* wouldn't," he said. He rolled his eyes when Hugo shot him an angry look. "There's someone singing in the water down there."

Hugo moved closer. "I don't hear anything."

"I do," Dru said. "Corinne heard a song in the water from this well, and here it is again."

"*La sirène?*" Hugo asked, looking worried.

Bouki shook his head. "No, the mermaids helped us."

"If it's not the mermaids, then who could be singing to children from under the water?" Hugo asked.

Bouki snapped his fingers. "Which jumbie likes to pretend to be things she is not?"

Pierre winced. "Severine."

"You and your child said she was gone," Mrs. Duval said. "You told us the whole cliff fell on top of her."

"And what," the witch asked, "made any of you think a whole cliff would be enough to kill Severine?"

42

Two Things

Corinne lay on the muddy bank of the lagoon, trying to catch her breath.

"You tried to drown me!" Laurent cried between fits of coughing. "Why, Corinne?"

Corinne wanted to explain. She pushed herself up, but Laurent cowered while Marlene and Gabrielle looked at her with wide, frightened eyes.

"Let's get the children home," Miss Evelyn said. She helped Laurent to his feet as two others picked up Marlene and Gabrielle.

"What about Corinne?" Marlene asked in her small voice.

"She doesn't care about you," Laurent said. "She doesn't care about any of us."

Marlene furrowed her brow. "But she wasn't with me at the well. It couldn't have been her."

"I didn't see anyone," Gabrielle said. "The water was singing to me."

"She was on the beach when I was taken," Laurent said. "I remember." His face twisted with disgust. Marlene slipped away and knelt in front of Corinne.

"Are you really a jumbie, Corinne? My mama said you were, but she also said you were my friend."

"I am a jumbie, and I am your friend, Marlene," Corinne said.

Corinne wasn't sure what she was, really. She had saved the children, but no one believed her. She was only a jumbie to them, as though there was no girl left in her. They looked at her with faces filled with anger, and fear, and loathing. The girl in her had made her *want* to help. But it was the jumbie in her that had saved the children.

Suddenly, a thick cloud covered the forest and the lagoon, plunging everything into deep darkness. To Corinne's right, a dim orange glow appeared beneath the mud. She dug until she turned up her mama's stone, still wrapped in leather. She pressed the mud-caked stone to her heart then took it to the water to wash it off.

"Look out, Corinne!" Marlene yelled.

Two long, splintery arms grabbed hold of Corinne and pulled her down. "Foolish child!" Severine said. "I know what you did!"

"You're too late," Corinne said. "I got them back to their parents."

Severine's eyes flashed. She let go of Corinne and made a swipe for Marlene. Miss Evelyn pulled the girl back as the other adults splashed into the water to fight off Severine. Severine swung her arms and knocked them over, then she caught Corinne's ankle and dragged her out. "You promised to keep them for me. So, who is the liar?"

"I'm sorry, Tante—"

"Do not call me that!" Severine screamed. Her eyes were wide and wild. "What kind of family is it that lies and deceives?"

"Ours," Corinne said. "You lied to me and Papa about who you were. Before that, Mama lied to him."

Severine dove on Corinne, pinning her under the water. Corinne kicked and scratched at Severine with her fingers, but her aunt was much too strong. The people in the crowd moved in, trying to pry Corinne from Severine's grip, but the jumbie held them off. She pulled Corinne deeper into the water.

Corinne put her mama's stone in her mouth. There was no way to fight Severine and win. She put her hands up to surrender. They both surfaced in the middle of the lagoon, far from the watching crowd. Corinne tied her mama's stone around her neck. Severine eyed it carefully.

"I have not figured out how the stone affects me so much more than it does you," Severine said. "Another thing my sister hid from me."

"We shouldn't fight," Corinne said. "We are family." Her fingers closed around the stone.

Severine backed off. "We are only family when you want to trick me."

"We are family whether either of us likes it or not," Corinne said. "We didn't get to choose that. But we can choose what kind of family we are together."

"You don't want what I want," the jumbie said. "You would use the gifts your mother gave you against jumbies—against your own kind."

In the water behind Severine, Malik's small brown face surfaced with the three mermaids. Her friends had come. Weren't they her kind, too? All of them?

"I don't have one kind," Corinne said. "I am my mother's child. I am my father's child, too. I don't have to choose."

"You do," Severine said. "Stupid girl, you always have to choose." Severine lunged forward but Sisi, Noyi, and Addie grabbed her.

Severine was surrounded.

43

The Water Jumbies

Severine twisted one way and then another, and all four of them spiraled down. The mermaids' flesh tore on Severine's hard skin as they struggled. Corinne grabbed Malik and tried to pull him away, but the undercurrent had caught him. Corinne took a deep breath and sank with him. She motioned for him to open his mouth, and she put her mama's stone inside it. The mermaids' thrashing churned the water, so Corinne could not feel the pulse of the current. Malik passed the stone back to her. She caught her breath and returned it. Corinne kept kicking for the surface, but the current sucked at them like a hungry mouth.

There was only one person who could help, but she would not come for Corinne and Malik. Maybe she would come for her children.

The mermaids are in trouble! Corinne called out.

A long tail undulated in and out of the water, slowly and gracefully. Mama D'Leau could not have been far. She stopped and cocked her head, watching Corinne and Malik struggle.

They cannot fight her, Corinne said. *They will not survive.*

I can't interfere with another jumbie business, Mama D'Leau said.

But they are jumbies, too, Corinne said.

They already paying for getting involved, Mama D'Leau said. *And that is your fault too, eh.*

Soil whipped up from the bottom of the lagoon. Corinne tasted scum. There was a pause in the fighting, and Corinne pushed Malik up to the surface and toward the shore. She stayed behind, treading water, with Severine beneath her, and Mama D'Leau between her and land.

"There is no way to stop her, then," Corinne said to Mama D'Leau.

Mama D'Leau merely twisted a plait around her finger.

Corinne chewed her lip. "But if she forgot herself, that could stop her." She narrowed her eyes at Mama D'Leau. "You made the mermaids forget once."

"Me?" she said. "When they reach across the water, I wasn't there to help them remember. So, you tell me how that work."

"They remembered who they were when they got close to home, and they forgot again when they were far away," Corinne said. "So it was the water that did it. Not you."

Mama D'Leau splashed the water with her tail.

"You can get her far enough away that she forgets," Corinne said.

"Why I should leave? This is your mess." Mama D'Leau leaned closer to Corinne. "Anyhow, no one want you here. They don't like you."

"They don't like you either," Corinne said.

"They have no choice but to respect me. But you . . ."

"They hate everything I do."

"It look like you hate yourself, too."

Corinne swallowed hard.

"You want that one there to forget. And you want to get away from all they hate and anger. So is you who should take her away. Not so?" Mama D'Leau smiled. "I can help you with that . . . if you ask me nice."

"My papa and my friends love me," Corinne said.

"But they don't understand," said Mama D'Leau. "They will never understand what it is to be you. How can they know what it feel like when someone look at you and hate you just for how you born?"

"But I will forget everything," Corinne said.

Mama D'Leau's face broke into a soft grin. Her eyes sparkled like moonlight on water. "What you want to remember, girl?"

Corinne thought of her mama's voice, and her father's hands, of Dru's smile, Bouki's jokes, Malik's cleverness, and Hugo's pastries. She remembered the smell of her garden, and the first sweet bite of orange, and the way the sea was like a lullaby. These were all things she loved and wanted to remember. And there were more.

But as long as Severine was after her and the entire island, everyone could lose the things they loved. What were Corinne's memories compared to the lives of everyone on the island? "Nothing," Corinne said. "I don't want to remember anything."

"One thing for sure, you won't get very far like that." Mama D'Leau waved her hand at Corinne's body. "Your friends below would never have survived if they had stayed girls."

"So you will change me, too," Corinne said.

"Yes. But I can't change you back," Mama D'Leau said. "I don't work so."

"Go ahead," Corinne said.

Mama D'Leau cocked an eyebrow.

Corinne added, "Please."

44

Just in Time

Bouki and Pierre arrived at the lagoon just in time to see Mama D'Leau block Corinne from the people on shore. Pierre dove into the water. Mama D'Leau pushed him back to land with her tail. Malik ran to Bouki.

"What happened, brother?" Bouki asked, but he didn't need Malik's answer to know that Corinne was in trouble.

45

Girl or Jumbie?

So you are a jumbie after all," Mama D'Leau said to Corinne. She put her hands on Corinne's shoulders and ran them down to her toes.

Corinne was surprised at how comforting the jumbie's warm hands were against her skin. "I'm a girl, too," she said.

Mama D'Leau backed away. "Not anymore."

Where Corinne's legs had been, a shimmering orange tail waved.

46

The Mermaid's Argument

Mama D'Leau moved aside and smiled as if she was presenting Corinne to the people on shore. Fear showed in their eyes, but also wonder. Corinne didn't feel any different, but when her tail flipped out of the water, and the people on shore shrank back, she knew that it didn't matter what she felt; they would always see her as something different. Bouki, Dru, and Malik stared, too, but unlike the others, she didn't see fear in their faces.

"Corinne!" Pierre called.

Mama D'Leau backed off so he could reach Corinne.

"Papa!" Corinne said.

"What did you do?" He dove at Mama D'Leau and managed to knock her under.

"No, Papa, please," Corinne said. She pulled Pierre out of Mama D'Leau's reach. "She didn't do this to hurt me. I asked her to."

"Why, Corinne?"

"Severine will not stop until she has what she wants. But if I take her far away, she will forget who she is, and all of you will be safe."

Pierre looked confused.

"It will be fine, Papa," she said. It was the first time she had ever lied to him. "The water washed away the mermaids' memories. It will do the same for Severine."

"She won't leave the island."

"You said she was greedy, Papa. She will leave if she thinks there is something to gain."

"Like what?"

"Me."

Pierre grabbed Corinne's wrist. "I won't let you go."

"You are not strong enough to stop me, Papa," Corinne said. She pulled away from him and floated on the surface for a moment. Behind Pierre, her friends looked confused and upset. Tears burned Corinne's eyes. She dove toward the mermaids and grabbed Severine's hand. *I choose to be your family,* Corinne said. *We will stay together, Tante.*

Severine narrowed her eyes.

We don't need a small island when we have the entire sea,
Corinne said. *It is huge and wide and deep.* Corinne sang:

Wide and deep and vast and blue,
Waves of gray that tumble through.
Leave this place, forget the past.
Peace waits in the waves at last.

Think how much we can do in the sea together, Tante.
Come.

47

Bitterness like Dew

Bouki couldn't move or speak as he watched Corinne transform and then disappear under the water. Pierre cried out. Mr. and Mrs. Rootsingh pulled Dru in close. Mrs. Duval squeezed Laurent against her body. Hugo kept a tight hold on Bouki and Malik. It was as if Pierre's sorrow might tear them all apart or as if Corinne's change was catching.

When Corinne resurfaced with Severine, Pierre swam after them. But the jumbies were faster, and they were long gone before Pierre reached the inlet that connected to the sea. His calls to Corinne echoed off the stumps of trees that lined the forest side of the lagoon, and the sharp, bare hill that closed the lagoon off on the other side.

Bouki didn't notice when Mama D'Leau disappeared, and he didn't know what happened to the mermaids. He held his brother's hand as the moon dipped and the surface of the lagoon stilled again. People shuffled off until only he, Malik, Hugo, the Rootsinghs, and the white witch remained.

Something on the water rippled toward them. The mermaids appeared, carrying Pierre. They brought him slowly to the arms of Hugo and Mr. Rootsingh, who waded out to waist-deep water to get him.

"He is exhausted," Sisi said. "He would not stop following her."

Pierre's eyes flicked open and he whispered something Bouki couldn't hear.

"I will sing to her," Sisi said. "Maybe she will come back on her own."

"That's not likely," said the white witch. "She did this to save us. She chose it."

"Mama D'Leau has to be able to change her back," Dru said. She splashed into the water and looked from the mermaids to the white witch. "Tell her to change Corinne back!" Mrs. Rootsingh tried to pull Dru away, but she shook her mother's hands off.

The white witch shook her head sadly. "This was Mama D'Leau's plan all along."

"Why would she want to get rid of Corinne?" Dru asked.

"It's not Corinne she wants to get rid of," said a leisurely voice behind them. Papa Bois stood on shore as if he had been there all along. "Two crabs can't share the same hole."

"You mean Severine and Mama D'Leau? But they weren't in the same hole," Bouki said. "One was on land, and the other was in the water."

"You really are a dunce," the witch said. "Severine wasn't on land anymore."

"What does that have to do with Corinne?" Dru asked. She ran to Papa Bois. "You can help her. You can make Mama D'Leau turn her back."

"Even Mama D'Leau can't help her now," Papa Bois said.

"She's not going to remember her family and her friends. She won't remember anything," Dru said. "There has to be something we can do."

"I will do anything," Pierre said.

"Here." Papa Bois handed a sack of seeds to Dru. "Plant these. You can help me get the forest back."

"How will that help Corinne?" Bouki asked.

"What is one creature against the hundreds who have lost their homes?" Papa Bois asked. "Corinne has made her choice, and we are left to do what we must without her." He returned slowly to the trees and disappeared the moment his hooves touched ground inside the mahogany forest.

Dru threw the sack down. "Not until you help my friend," she yelled into the forest. "You said that she was responsible for the first fire, too. You said that both of us would have to pay. How can she do what you ask if she's a mermaid?"

Mrs. Rootsingh scooped Dru into her arms. Mr. Rootsingh picked up the sack. They nodded to Pierre, Hugo, and the witch and went home.

The witch turned toward the swamp. Hugo and the boys walked with Pierre back the way they had come, over the crisp ash of the forest floor, until they reached the road that led to the sea in one direction and to town in the other.

"Go home, friend," Pierre said. "I am fine from here."

"No. We will come with you," Bouki said.

When they came to the point in the road where the first glimpse of the sea was visible over the hill, Pierre faltered. Hugo reached out and grabbed his arm. The four of them stood in the moonlight looking over the sparkling water. Bitterness settled on Pierre like dew. Bouki wondered if Corinne's papa would ever love the sea again.

48

Where Water Turns to Stone

Corinne felt her papa's heartbeat reaching out to her as she swam. Then, as she went past some gliding turtles, Corinne stopped feeling its strong beat. She swam past her own beach and out to the wider sea, over the large coral fields and under the clouds of sargassum. Then she turned south. She didn't want to go the same way that the mermaids had gone. She didn't want their memories to cloud her own. She wanted a new place, one where she and Severine would forget.

Where are we going? Severine asked.

We'll know when we get there, Corinne told her.

Severine's eyes were wide with wonder as Corinne pulled her along. She asked questions about each thing they passed, and Corinne answered gently, as if Severine was a child in her charge. She told her about the turtles, and the manatees, and the coral, about the whales, and the fish that lit up like fireflies in the depths of the sea.

The water turned colder, but Corinne didn't react to its chill. She pushed on, letting it wash over her, until she was far enough away that she barely remembered warm water or a small green island under the sun. As they swam, a soft melody came across the water.

Mmm siren, mmm doux doux,
Don't go too far, come home soon.
Mmm cherie, mmm child,
Don't ship yourself to the wild.
They love you here, they long to see you,
Their open arms are out to greet you.
Mmm siren, mmm doux doux,
Come home, come home, come soon.

What is that? Severine asked. *It's pretty.*

Corinne swam faster and tried to cover the mermaids' song with her own.

Tante siren, Tante esprit,
The waves wash our memories clean.
Tante doux doux, Tante cherie,
Lost within this world of green.
The waves of memory crash above us,
Our salty tears wash away.
Mmm Tante, Tante doux doux,
Come away, come away, yes do.

The mermaids' song changed again:

Remember us in distant shores,
Remember us forevermore.
Our love breaks from wave to wave,
Your tears trace the path you pave.
Hand to hand and heart to heart,
Love can never be torn apart.
Heart to heart and hand to hand,
From water's chill to sun-warmed sand.

The song went around and through Corinne as she swam farther into the cold, clear water, where pieces of the sea hardened to ice and floated around them. She had a fuzzy memory of a boy sitting by the water listening to the waves. *Remember us in distant shores. Remember us forevermore.* Maybe the song was for him.

Where are we? Severine asked. *Are we home?*

Corinne looked at the cold, white world around them. She didn't know where they were, or how they had come here, or why. She pulled her hand away from Severine's. *Who are you?* she asked.

The twiggy creature frowned. *Who are you?* she asked back.

The mermaid looked at her brown skin and orange tail. She didn't know.

49

The Usual

Bouki shuffled behind the long bristles of a cocoyea broom, sweeping the path in front of the bakery. Dough was just rising in the hot oven and its smell mingled with the scent of milky tea.

Marlene walked down the main road with small determined steps. She didn't look at Bouki when he waved. "Where are you going?" he asked.

"To get Corinne," she said.

"You can't," Bouki said.

Marlene didn't stop. All she said was, "She came for me."

Bouki called Malik. They followed her to Corinne's

house, and when no one answered the door, they went around to the back. Pierre was looking over the beach. The other fishermen had long pushed out to sea. Their boats bobbed in the waves like toys.

"What was it like under the sea?" Pierre asked.

"It was enormous," Bouki said. And then, "Beautiful, too."

"The water is dangerous," Pierre said. "It's like a monster waiting to open its maw and swallow you whole. I've seen the monster wake up."

Marlene tugged at Pierre's shirt. "Corinne's papa?" she said. "I brought these for Corinne. They are her favorite." She handed him a bottle of her mama's red plums.

Pierre went down on one knee to take it from her. "Does your mama know where you are?"

She popped a thumb into her mouth and nodded. Then her eyes turned to the ground and she shook her head.

"You know Corinne is not home."

"She will come back for that," Marlene said. "Put it in the water. Mama told me people put gifts in the sea and that's how I came back."

"I don't think it will work," Pierre said.

Marlene slipped a thin gold band off her wrist and held it out to him. "You can have that, too." She got up to her tiptoes and whispered, "Everybody likes lots of presents."

Pierre clutched the plums and kissed Marlene on the top of her head. People in the fishing village looked up at them. Laurent waved, and Mrs. Duval rubbed his head.

Bouki sighed. "We're going to have to fix this ourselves."

"I can help?" Marlene asked.

"You already did," Bouki said. "Let's go. And bring that with you."

Marlene replaced her bracelet and stood up taller.

• • •

They found the Rootsinghs at the edge of the forest pushing seeds past the ash and into the ground. They stopped planting when the boys and Marlene got close.

"What's the plan?" Dru asked.

"Tangling with jumbies, getting into dangerous spots, doing all the things you are not supposed to do. You know, the usual," Bouki said.

"We are supposed to be helping Papa Bois," Dru said.

Mr. Rootsingh waved them on. "I'm not sure how much help it is to plant so soon. The earth needs time to heal. But I am no jumbie. What do I know?"

Malik went to Mrs. Rootsingh and whispered. She reached down and unhinged the gold anklet that tinkled when she walked. She dropped it into his palm.

"We're going to need more than my mama's anklet," Dru said. "We're going to need almost everyone on the island."

"I get the feeling Papa Bois only wants us to plant so he can teach us a lesson," Mr. Rootsingh said. "He does not need our help to regrow the forest."

"We're all going then?" Dru asked.

"We don't want you to get into any trouble," Mrs. Rootsingh said. "None of you."

"Why does everyone look at me when they say the word *trouble?*" Bouki complained.

By the end of the day, a noisy crowd led by children gathered in Pierre's front yard. Dru explained the plan. Pierre brought the bottle of red plums and picked a flower from the plant that grew up between the roots of Corinne's orange tree. He followed Dru to the beach. The crowd was boisterous and chatty, like a carnival parade. Large banana leaves fanned their shoulders, and there were colorful gifts in their upturned palms. The children held tiny bracelets and earrings, rag dolls and wire cars, cricket bats made from coconut branches, and cork balls with perfect stitching.

Behind them, their parents came with more jewelry, silver-handled combs, hairpins, and embroidered fabric. Last of all came the white witch. She hobbled behind with nothing but her walking stick and a tired frown.

They lined up on the wet sand and waited as the sun dove toward the sea, washing everything in soft orange light. The moment the sun touched the top of the water, they set the banana leaves with their gifts on the waves and pushed them into the surf.

People from the fishing village came to join them. They took off their earrings and bracelets and necklaces and tossed them into the sea. Laurent tugged Mrs. Duval forward. She unhooked a delicate gold chain from her throat and threw it into the crest of a wave. Laurent squeezed her hand.

The gifts gleamed in the sunset as they floated on the leaves and sank in the water.

Pierre put Corinne's flower in the water and pushed it gently out. It looked like a spark of fire. He put the bottle of plums down. It lodged in the sand, where the waves pushed sand around it, burying it slowly.

The sun had nearly disappeared, and still nothing happened.

"It isn't working," Bouki said.

The witch sighed. She rubbed her withered arm and moved up.

"Not you," a slow, creaking voice said. The crowd made way for Papa Bois. "You have sacrificed enough, witch," he said. He stepped in front of her and took out Mama D'Leau's stone. He held it up to the last remaining light, then touched it to the delicate froth that was retreating to the sea.

Mama D'Leau rose out of the water and rode to them on a wave like a throne. When it broke, she towered over them with the end of her tail flicking sea foam. "Is rare that you call me," she said to Papa Bois.

"I have been reminded that the girl owes me a debt," he said.

"So?" Mama D'Leau shrugged.

"So you have taken someone who has promised to work for me," he said. "That's not our way. She will have to come back."

"I didn't take her," Mama D'Leau said. "She left her own self."

Papa Bois dipped his head. "With some help from you, I think." He pointed his stick back at the island. "You can have her back after she has helped the forest regrow."

"If you making them do it on they own, it will take forever," Mama D'Leau said.

Papa Bois smiled. The wrinkles around his eyes creased. "How will they learn?" he asked. "And anyway, what is time to us?"

"I don't know where she gone to," Mama D'Leau said. "She was determined, eh? She would have gotten far already."

"You can reach anything in the water," he said. "You can find her."

"What she go come back for? She won't remember anything by now. Why she would want to come back to things she don't know?"

"Take me," Pierre said. "She will remember me."

"She won't," Dru said. "She is too far from home."

"I am her home," Pierre said. He walked into the water and plucked Corinne's flower out of the waves as he went.

Mama D'Leau dove in an arc backward into the sea. Her tail curved into the air casting flecks of glittering foam over the crowd. The tip of it wrapped around Pierre and pulled him down.

50

A Spark of Memory

The shadow bore down on them fast in the freezing cold water, splitting them apart as they moved to get out of the way. The thick black-and-white fish turned sharply, its jaws open and its teeth as white as the ice floating in the water around them.

It won't stop, the mermaid said. *We have to go different ways.*

The twig creature nodded and darted off in another direction. It was surprisingly fast despite having no fins. The fish stuck with the mermaid. It moved its smooth body through the water easily and snapped at the end of her tail. The mermaid dove abruptly, then doubled back, hoping to shake it off, but the fish was nearly as agile as she was and came after her again, this time diving deep and coming from below.

It hit her with its nose and sent her rolling against a block of ice. Some of the ice splintered off. The mermaid grabbed a large shard and charged at the fish as it came at her again. She dug the shard of ice into the fish's side, but its skin was so tough, there was little damage. She left the ice wedged in its flesh and readied herself to take it head-on, but it darted behind a floe. The mermaid stopped. A steady heartbeat rippled across the water and bounced against her skin.

Corinne, came a voice.

The mermaid turned. A man with long hair and sad brown eyes faced her. She lifted her hand and then remembered that she no longer had the shard of ice to defend herself. She fled. The man followed, carried by a creature with ice-cold eyes that was much larger than he was. The pair matched the mermaid's every move. She dove down, and they dove with her. She turned, and they turned.

She gave up and faced them, ready to fight, but the man held his arms open. In one hand was a small, bright thing, the color of her tail. She thought she had seen something like it before, but where? She lived in a world of ice. She darted toward the man, and at the last moment, he moved aside and pressed his hand to hers. As their skin touched, it sparked a memory. It was the sound of laughter. She pulled away with the small orange and yellow flower in her hand, and the laughter rang through her mind again. It was her own laughter, and the man's too. She frowned and swam away again.

This time the man and the creature with him didn't follow. The man called out, *Grand-père is king of the fish-folk and I have seawater in my veins.*

And I am my mama's child, the mermaid said. *I belong on the land.* She remembered saying this every morning to the man, but she could not recall where. When she looked at him again, it was a face she knew. She stopped swimming.

Corinne.

Papa?

Corinne's heart began to fill with memories of her papa, her friends, and her island. They flooded her like sunlight. Moment after lovely moment sparkled and bounced through her. But there were clouds on the edges of her mind. She swam away with her papa, but she kept looking back. There was something else she had forgotten. Or someone. In the distance, a shape like a bundle of twigs drifted. Corinne reached out, but it was too far away.

51

Turning Back

Corinne pushed up out of the water and slung the piece of net into the little yellow boat, while still hanging on to the edge. On the other side of the boat was her beach and her house just above it, on the hill. Pierre pulled her from the warm water. She landed on top of the nets, getting one of her feet caught.

"Are you going to stay out here all morning?" Pierre asked.

"You need my help, Papa," Corinne said, extracting her foot.

"I don't mind the company," her papa said. "And it's always a good strategy to drum up demand for your business by making your customers wait. But they won't wait forever." He winked and looked up at their house where her orange tree was laden with fruit. "Anyway, if you wait too long, all the fruit will rot, and then you won't be the girl with the sweetest oranges on the island anymore."

Corinne kissed Pierre's rough face. She looked for the worry that sometimes played behind his eyes, and couldn't find it. "Okay, Papa," she said. She dove off the side of the boat and swam to the beach, then trudged up the hill to change her clothes and fill her basket before heading to town.

Corinne passed the dry well and then the full well with the mahogany forest to her right. The trees still looked like sharp, black shadows, but a few green shoots were already pushing up between them. When she arrived at the market, she maneuvered around noisy vendors holding out fruit and vegetables and scooting back chickens that were trying to make their escape. She came to her usual spot. Miss Evelyn and Miss Aileen had kept a space open for her. Mrs. Rootsingh and Dru had already set up to her left.

"You came!" Dru said.

Corinne quietly spread out her blanket. "Good morning, Miss Evelyn, Miss Aileen."

The women nodded and smiled only slightly, as if any more would crack their faces.

Dru helped set up the oranges in pyramids of five.

Corinne noticed Dru staring at her legs again. "I'm not going to turn," Corinne said.

"How are you so sure?" Dru asked.

The truth was, Corinne didn't know exactly how she had become a girl again. As Mama D'Leau had pulled her and Pierre through the sea, her memories had slowly returned, and she had wished she could be a girl again. She wanted to be with her papa on land and run with her friends over the rocky hills. The desire tingled along her spine and extended up and down her body. But the tingling reminded her of something else—that feeling she got when people were watching her. She had looked around and found the eyes of several other mermaids lined up in the sea.

They floated shoulder to shoulder, hands clasped and colorful tails waving beneath their bodies. Their faces were dark as shadows, all different, but each one beautiful. Corinne's heart swelled. She had been wrong. Mama D'Leau had long ago saved more than the four mermaids who carried her and her friends across the sea. She had not left them all to perish. As Corinne was pulled along, the mermaids began to sing in a language that Corinne didn't know. Their hearts beat out a steady rhythm and their words undulated like a wave cresting and crashing and cresting again.

She looked at Mama D'Leau and her papa, but Mama D'Leau was focused on the sea ahead, and her papa only had eyes for Corinne. They didn't see the mermaids who lined the way, and they didn't seem to hear the song that followed them home.

By the time they arrived, Corinne was a girl again. She didn't know how, and the look of surprise on Mama D'Leau's face told Corinne that the jumbie didn't know, either.

Corinne and Dru continued to stack the oranges. As the fruits rubbed against each other, their scent rose and mingled with the other smells of the market, peppery, spicy, earthy smells that made Corinne wish for a snack. Marlene tapped her shoulder lightly and held out a piece of brown paper with five plums inside. Corinne took them and Marlene threw her arms around Corinne's neck and hugged her hard. Then she chose two oranges, held up two fingers, and skipped off to her mother. Mrs. Chow smiled and waved and brushed Marlene's already smooth hair with her fingers. Corinne shared the plums with Dru.

Vendors called out, "Bananas for a dollar! Sweet like no other!" and "Plenty fruit, fat and douce!" Buyers swarmed Corinne, buying pyramid after pyramid of her oranges.

"See?" Dru said. "No one is afraid of you."

"They're barely talking to me though," Corinne observed.

"They are buying. That's what's important," Mrs. Rootsingh said. "It doesn't matter what anybody else thinks of you. It only matters what you think of yourself."

Across the market, Corinne spotted Mrs. Ramdeen with her basket hooked onto her arm. She looked small and frail as she walked through the vendors, buying only a few things. She took up the tiniest pile of bodi and the smallest of the christophene. Her eyes flicked toward Corinne and flicked away again. She avoided Corinne's side of the market entirely.

Corinne was about to hop over her oranges toward Mrs. Ramdeen when Dru caught her arm. "I have to do something, Dru," Corinne protested.

"What can you do? The douens would not let Allan go."

"We got everyone else home. Why can't we get him back too?" Corinne passed out her few remaining oranges to Mrs. Rootsingh, Miss Evelyn, and Miss Aileen and grabbed her basket. Dru followed her out of the market. "Maybe I can find someone to get him back."

Along the road, Bouki and Malik fell into step next to them. "Where are we off to?" Bouki asked.

"I don't know," Dru said.

"When do we ever know what we're doing, eh, brother?" Bouki asked Malik, giving him a nudge. Malik nudged him back harder.

Corinne turned into the mahogany forest. She pulled Bouki's slingshot out of his pocket and placed a stone against the strap, then pulled it back and squinted one eye as she looked around for something to shoot.

"You don't really mean to do that, do you?" A stump to the right of them unfolded itself and Papa Bois sat cross-legged in the middle of a few tiny sprouts.

Corinne smiled. "No, sir."

Papa Bois bowed his head. "Come. Work." He handed them seeds, which they began to plant around him.

"Papa," Corinne said as she worked. "Mama D'Leau said she couldn't change me back from a mermaid, but when I got here, I was a girl again."

"Yes."

"And what about Ellie? She was one of the mermaids. She changed back into a girl when she tried to go home. Only she didn't survive. How come?"

"What do you think?" Papa Bois asked.

Corinne pushed a few seeds into the soil. "I think when I remembered who I was, I wanted to go home. And when Ellie remembered who she was, she wanted to go home, too."

"Right," Papa Bois said.

"But Ellie died. And I became me again."

"Ellie had been with Mama D'Leau a long time. Centuries," Papa Bois said. "You human saplings don't last very long. Not without some help."

"So it's not too late for Allan, then?" Dru asked.

"Your little douen friend?" Papa Bois said. "That depends."

"On what?" Bouki asked.

Corinne sat back on her heels. "It depends on whether he wants to go back or not. That was the thing that changed Ellie and me, wasn't it? We both wanted to go home."

Papa Bois smiled at her. His kind eyes warmed her right through. "Only your friend can choose to come back," he said. "Everyone has the power to be the thing they most want. Your little friend is going to have to want it so badly that there is no other choice but to change."

"He's afraid," Dru said.

Corinne put her hand on Dru's shoulder. "We will have to remind him of the things he loves. He won't be afraid then."

Papa Bois pointed his walking stick to a path in the forest. Dru ran ahead, calling Allan's name. They found him scratching with a twig at the gray soil beneath a burned-out tree.

Dru dropped to her knees in front of him. "Allan? Do you want to be a boy again?"

He nodded.

"You can go home if you want to," Corinne said.

Allan continued to dig.

"Do you remember the things you loved?" Corinne asked. "Like pelau."

"And goat's milk," Dru added.

Malik made a circle in the dirt and pitched a stone into it.

"Marbles," Bouki said.

Allan smiled.

"And your soft bed?" Dru added.

Allan stood.

"Come on," Corinne said.

Bouki stepped in front of them. "Are you sure you want a mother?" he asked. "It might be better without one. They are very fussy."

Allan walked around Bouki. He kept a quick, steady pace all the way to the market, hurrying ahead of the others, even on his backward jumbie feet. Mrs. Ramdeen was finishing up her shopping.

"Mama!" he called out.

Mrs. Ramdeen dropped her basket. The bodi fanned out, and the green christophene fell to the ground and rolled and bounced over the dirt. Her eggs broke and yolk traced a path from Mrs. Ramdeen's toes toward Allan's heels.

The market hushed.

Allan took a few wobbly steps toward his mama. He paused and turned back to Dru. She nodded and Corinne waved him on.

"Remember who you are," Corinne said.

"Only if you really want," Bouki added.

Corinne stomped Bouki's foot.

Allan took a step backward, closer to his mama.

"Remember how you used to follow me everywhere?" Dru asked. "Remember how we used to swap our marbles? Remember how your mama used to sing to you at night?"

Allan took another step.

"Turn around, Allan," Corinne said. "All you have to do is want to go home."

Allan turned toward his mama again. This time, his feet didn't move, so his body lined up perfectly. When he stepped forward, his movement was steady and sure.

Mrs. Ramdeen dropped to her knees. Allan ran into her arms and they cried against each other's cheeks.

Corinne's heart felt full. The melody of the mermaids' song that had accompanied her home played in her memory. She threw her head back, and felt the sun on her face, and laughed. As she and her friends left the market, the crowd closed in behind them, surrounding Allan and his mother.

"You saved all of them, Corinne!" Dru said.

Corinne blushed. "I couldn't have done it without all of you."

"I wonder if you and Allan can switch back if you want to?" Bouki asked. "This jumbie thing could be useful sometimes."

Corinne shook her head.

"What do you like better? Being a jumbie or being a girl?" he asked.

"I like being Corinne."

"And it means you can be on land and in the sea," Dru said.

Corinne stopped walking.

"What is it?" Dru asked.

"Severine," she said. "I left her behind."

"Good riddance," said Bouki. He high-fived Malik.

"She doesn't know who she is, or even where she is. She's lost and alone."

"I thought that was the idea," Bouki said.

"I told her I would stay with her," Corinne said.

Dru rubbed Corinne's arm. "There's nothing you can do now. She wanted to hurt all of us. Isn't this better?"

Malik touched Corinne's hand and pointed to his head.

"I know she doesn't remember now," Corinne said. "But what if she does later? I remembered who I was. Ellie did too. And Allan. What if her memory comes back?"

"How?" Bouki asked. "Ellie remembered because she was sent home. You remembered because your father went for you. And Allan only needed to know that he could go home if he wanted to. There's no one to remind Severine." He swiped his hands twice as if he was dusting the very idea off his palms.

"I would worry more about Mama D'Leau," Dru said.

"She's not as bad as she seems," Corinne said.

"True," said Bouki.

"You never told us why she let you go," Dru said.

Bouki grinned. "I probably talked too much."

Dru giggled, but Corinne caught a look from Bouki that told her he was hiding something.

"Anyway, I don't know why you are worried about jumbies in the sea when there is one right here on land causing trouble," he continued. "Everywhere she goes is trouble!" He slapped Corinne's shoulder and jogged ahead. Dru and Malik joined him, all of them grinning. "Tag!" he called out as he peeled off.

Corinne took a deep breath. Maybe they were right. Maybe there was nothing to worry about. "You know I'm faster than you on land or in the water," she said. They crested the hill and the sea came into view below them. It was deep, and vast, and beautiful. And for all the trouble it hid beneath, she loved it still.

Acknowledgments

I like to think of all the many, many people I rely on to produce a story as Team Tracey. Or Team Jumbie. (Which is the same thing, really.) Up first is Darryl Baptiste, who is the MVP of this team, keeping me in chocolates, oysters, and gentle doses of reality as (very often) needed. My mom, Gloria Regis-Hosein, is always there to remind me that if J. K. Rowling can make billions, I CAN TOO. She also makes stellar meals and pulls me back on track when I go off the rails. My dad, Roland Hosein, is ever available for grammar and Trini fact-checking, which he takes on with the enthusiasm of a dog with a bone. I wouldn't be here without the support of my agent, Marie Lamba, and the entire JDLA team.

The entire Ghana section was vetted with the help of Nathalie Mvondo, Nana Asare, Godwin Danso, and Kofi Gyasi. Turns out the Twi language is as tricky as any jumbie.

I'd also like to thank Team Algonquin Young Readers, especially my editors, Elise Howard (who is part fairy godmother and part mythical genius) and Sarah Alpert (who understands about the commas), for making me look good. Eileen Lawrence, Brooke Csuka, and Trevor Ingerson make marketing, publicity, and author-wrangling look like a breeze! (They're not.) Thank you and virtual hugs to Vivienne To, whose cover art literally made me cry.

I wouldn't have the totally stress-free career that this writing-for-children thing is without a guild of brassy, brave, generous women. Thanks especially to my own fleet of mermaids—Olugbemisola Rhuday-Perkovich, Renée Watson, Ibi Zoboi, Jennifer Baker, and Dhonielle Clayton—for swimming with me in this often-choppy ocean and doing it with grace.

Finally, I'd like to thank my children, Alyssa and Adam, and also Barkley, for the very useful advice, crazy story ideas, excellent jokes, warm hugs, wet kisses, and the fur and grape jelly in my writing chair. I hope you guys like this one, too. Just remember to hand-sell this book to all your friends or Mommy won't feed you.

xo